JOKE AND DAGGER

THE WORST DETECTIVE EVER, BOOK 8

CHRISTY BARRITT

D1506284

River Heights

COMPLETE BOOK LIST

Squeaky Clean Mysteries:

#14 Cold Case: Clean Sweep

#15 Cold Case: Clean Break

#16 Cleans to an End

While You Were Sweeping, A Riley Thomas Spinoff

The Sierra Files:

#1 Pounced

#2 Hunted

#3 Pranced

#4 Rattled

The Gabby St. Claire Diaries (a Tween Mystery series):

#1 The Curtain Call Caper

#2 The Disappearing Dog Dilemma

#3 The Bungled Bike Burglaries

The Worst Detective Ever

#1 Ready to Fumble

#2 Reign of Error

#3 Safety in Blunders

#4 Join the Flub

#5 Blooper Freak

#6 Flaw Abiding Citizen

#7 Gaffe Out Loud

#8 Joke and Dagger

#1 Edge of Peril

#2 Margin of Error

#3 Brink of Danger

#4 Line of Duty

#5 Legacy of Lies

#6 Secrets of Shame

#7 Refuge of Redemption

Cape Thomas Series:

#1 Dubiosity

#2 Disillusioned

#3 Distorted

Standalone Romantic Mystery:

The Good Girl

Suspense:

Imperfect

The Wrecking

Sweet Christmas Novella:

Home to Chestnut Grove

Standalone Romantic-Suspense:

Keeping Guard

The Last Target

Race Against Time

Ricochet

Key Witness

Lifeline

High-Stakes Holiday Reunion

Desperate Measures

Hidden Agenda

Mountain Hideaway

Dark Harbor

Shadow of Suspicion

The Baby Assignment

The Cradle Conspiracy

Trained to Defend

Mountain Survival

Dangerous Mountain Rescue

Nonfiction:

Characters in the Kitchen

Changed: True Stories of Finding God through Christian Music (out of print)

The Novel in Me: The Beginner's Guide to Writing and Publishing a Novel (out of print)

CHAPTER
ONE

"OH, JOEY. YOU LOOK HIDEOUS."

I cast a dirty look at Alistair King as I stepped out of the trailer where I'd just had my makeup done. "I'm supposed to look hideous, so I take that as a compliment."

My dad had taught me that life hack. When someone insults you, don't let them know it bothers you and they'll leave you alone.

I paused on the steps, waiting to hear what else Alistair had to say. Because, whether I wanted to or not, I was going to hear it. As director and producer, he *was* officially my boss for the next two weeks. The good news was that the only people who would see me like this were the cast and crew of *A Useless Ending to a Hard-Fought Life.*

Otherwise, this location that had been chosen for

filming should keep me isolated from the rest of the world and safely away from the vultures I called the media.

"You don't understand." Alistair turned away from me, as if repulsed. "I didn't expect Mindy to do such a good job. I mean, your startling bad looks are so realistic. You will not age well."

I licked my teeth—my false teeth, which had skillfully been stained brown and yellow. "I don't even know what to say to that."

"Oh, there's nothing you can say. Absolutely nothing." Alistair pressed his lips together, the edges of his mouth pulling back again in repugnance. Finally, he waved to the crew in the distance. "Let's just get on set."

I watched him as he walked away, and I shook my head.

Alistair King had curly dark hair that poofed atop his head. He reminded me somewhat of Prince. Or was it the Artist Formerly Known as Prince? You know, now that I thought about it, maybe he was now the artist formerly known as the Artist Formerly Known as Prince.

I couldn't keep up with these things.

Alistair was the producer and director of the new movie I was filming here in Lantern Beach, North Carolina. The location was secluded—so secluded you had to take two ferries to get here. But it was beautiful, especially this swath of land. The area jutted out into the water, with an old lighthouse sitting on the tip of the weathered landscape.

As I took a step forward, my thighs rubbed together. Well, not my actual thighs. I was wearing a suit that made me look about fifty pounds heavier.

In truthfulness, at times my actual thighs did brush each other. Whenever I noticed, it usually triggered a crash diet.

I hadn't been able to look at myself in the mirror since Mindy finished transforming me into a seventy-five-year-old woman who'd let herself go. I knew, deep down inside, part of me was more vain than I wanted to admit. I didn't know if I could stomach seeing how I would look with all my newly added imperfections. On a good day—without the suit, the makeup, the added wrinkles, and the false teeth—I was my own worst critic.

Alistair had insisted he needed someone self-confident for this new role in his upcoming movie. I must have everyone fooled because self-confident was not the word I would use to describe myself.

I ignored the stares from the crew as I walked from the row of trailers set up on the perimeter of the space. I had my own moderately sized RV. Production also had one, as well as hair and makeup. The rest of the cast and crew had what was called a triple banger or honeywagon. Basically, it was like an RV that had been divided into hotel rooms—one for each actor and a bathroom for everyone else.

I strode across the sand toward the crew in the distance.

Today was the first day of filming for an indie movie about a retired spy who had moved to an isolated island to grow old and die alone. However, the CIA needed her help to track down one of her old informants—at least, until the bitter end. I won't spoil it for you. Not yet, at least.

I was in between shooting new episodes of my hit TV show, *Relentless*, and my next big blockbuster-type of movie was still three months away from filming. Some people might call that a break and take a vacation. Me? I signed on to do this indie film.

Alistair was the man who'd first taken a chance on me when I was a nobody in Hollywood. He'd called to see if I would play this part in his upcoming movie and had sent me the script. After reading the first few pages, I knew this could be my breakout role.

This movie would never be a commercial success. But it would contain sweeping cinematography, thought-provoking dialogue, and a hopeless ending.

In other words, everyone would hate it—everyone except the critics.

Doing a more serious role like this had been on my bucket list for a while now. Then again, so has having a pedicure where fish ate the dead skin off my feet. Not all my bucket list items were good ideas.

I paused near the production crew and breathed in the fresh air. It was October, but it felt like the summer—until the wind blew, at least. But the sun shone brightly overhead, the waves crashed in the distance, and the fresh scent of the ocean promised that it was a good day for a good day.

"Okay, we need the lighthouse in the background." Alistair circled his hand in the air as he called us to order with the dramatic flair he was known for. "The structure plays an integral role in this story. Don't forget that. It symbolizes how ugly things can be beautiful as well as useful in a society that values attractiveness and youth."

No one could forget. Alistair had only repeated it about fifty times. The man was . . . exacting, to put it mildly. His head seemed to have gotten bigger since I'd last worked with him. Maybe it was because he was more experienced.

I took a quick minute to get myself in the zone. My mind fluttered through all the pages of script I'd tried to memorize. Alistair had sent an updated version last night, which hadn't made me happy. But as boss he called the shots, so I'd do what he asked—to an extent, of course. Any self-respecting actor had boundaries.

I took my position on the steps of the lighthouse. In a moment, I'd burst inside and start my lines. No doubt there was already a camera rolling inside, waiting for my grand entrance.

"Everyone in place!" Alistair yelled, clapping his hands.

People scrambled around me, moving as if they were afraid to poke the bear.

Alistair quieted. Waited three seconds for good measure. And then yelled, "And, action."

I instantly snapped into the mind-set of my character.

Washington George—yes, that was what he claimed was his real name, even though no one believed him—was my costar. The up-and-coming actor was only twenty-one, and he looked like a young Cary Grant. He'd yet to see me like this.

I wondered if on camera was the best time for it to happen. Then again, Alistair liked "organic acting" as he called it.

Fully immersed in the character of Drusilla Fairweather, I stared up at the lighthouse. Forcing myself to look pensive, I slowly climbed the steps.

I paused at the doorway, my hand on the handle. I took one last glance behind me, as if I feared being followed. I had a lot of real-life experience to tap into for that emotion.

Finally, after a moment of dramatic thought, where I'd actually found myself thinking about the plight of the seagull, I opened the door. I froze. Then I screamed and nearly tumbled backward.

Washington George lay at the base of the stairs.

Dead.

With blood pooling around his head and trickling from his mouth.

CHAPTER
TWO

I'D KNOWN I was going to see a dead body. But Mindy had done an excellent job making Washington's death look all too real.

I took a step back, remaining in character. But before I could deliver the lines I'd been practicing all night, I heard Alistair behind me.

"Cut! Cut! Cut!" He stormed toward me, his cheeks red and sand flying up behind his shoes with every step. "What in the world is going on, Joey? Have you lost your mind?"

I stared at him, wondering why he was so upset. I hadn't even said anything yet. "What do you mean?"

"This isn't in the script." He threw his hands in the air, his version of a volcano blowing its top. After the initial burst of emotion, he stared at me accusingly.

"Of course it is. I spent all night studying it. You added this scene here." I'd re-read the revisions about a million times, my resentment growing with each new line I'd memorized.

"No, of course I didn't. Why would you say that? Has that makeup done something to your brain?" He jammed his index finger into his temple and his eyes bulged.

My mouth dropped open, and I felt my chin—all three of them—bunch against my neck. "I could ask you the same question."

Before Alistair could retort, Washington sat up from his place on the floor, looking like the dead come back to life. "She's right, man. The new script you sent added this scene. I thought it was weird too."

"What in the world are you talking about? What new script? I don't change scripts like Zsa Zsa Gabor changed husbands." Heat came off Alistair like waves vaporizing from a blacktop in the middle of summer. "This must be some kind of joke."

Washington and I exchanged a look.

"You emailed it to us last night," I reminded Alistair, keeping my voice calm. "It had changes that we needed to memorize by today. *Or else.*"

I resisted an eye roll. The producer/director was

known for being dramatic. Those had been his words.

"Have you all lost your minds? I didn't do that. Why would I do that? In fact, when have I *ever* done that?" Alistair threw his hands in the air, histrionics full-blown.

Alistair's assistant, Sarah, stepped forward. "I got the revised script too."

Maybe hearing a third person say it made the rest of us seem less crazy.

Alistair ran a hand over his face and took a step back. "Someone is trying to sabotage my movie," he muttered. "That's what it has to be. Nothing else makes sense."

"Why would someone do that?" I wasn't a professional detective, but people mistook me for one all the time. I had years of experience pretending to be someone who was brilliant. Certainly some of that had worn off on the real me. Maybe I could help here.

"There are people out there who don't want to see me succeed," Alistair said. "Need I say more?"

Actually, well . . . yes. He would need to say more. If he wanted answers, at least.

"Let me see this new script." Alistair closed his eyes and held out his hand. I half expected him to tap his foot and demand a cigar while he was at it.

Sarah pulled out her phone and showed him the screen. He scrolled through. Grunting. Scowling. Scoffing.

Finally, he gave Sarah her phone back.

"I didn't send this." He pointed his nose up in the air.

He had said that several times. But the question was, if he didn't then who did? Who had access to a digital form of this script as well as his email?

And why? Maybe that was the biggest question of all. It made no sense that someone would go through all this trouble. But they had.

I had a bad feeling in my gut—a feeling that this was about more than a changed script.

It all had the markings of a really extravagant joke.

Or a sinister plot involving a fake murder.

An hour later, Alistair, Washington, and I had gathered for a meeting with the local police chief. We'd met in the production trailer. The three of us sat on a long couch while the police chief sat across from us at the kitchen table.

Even though Alistair would only be using this RV for a couple weeks, I noted that he'd added a lava lamp, some leopard-print pillows, and a stuffed jackalope. I supposed those personal items made this feel like a home away from home.

I personally thought calling in the local police was overkill, but Alistair had insisted that we take a break from filming to discuss this.

What did I know? I was merely a measly actress who was lending my name to this production as a favor to Alistair. I was also the one who had only two weeks to film this before I had to be back on the set of *Relentless*.

The police chief, Cassidy Chambers, looked like someone who could be in movies herself. She was thin with long, wavy blonde hair and sun-kissed skin. But when she spoke, her voice held the air of authority.

"So, you think someone is trying to sabotage this film?" Chief Chambers leaned back in her chair, and her gaze drifted from Alistair to Washington to me.

I supposed that we were the three principal players here. All in all, six different people had received the new script for last night.

"Is there anyone you can think of who might do this as a joke?" Chief Chambers asked.

"I can think of any number of people who might want to ruin me!" Alistair threw his hands into the air again, nearly slapping me as he did so. He really should've been an actor. He had the dramatic chops for it.

"Can you name a few of them for me?" Chief Chambers didn't crack a smile. In fact, I couldn't read what she was feeling. Irritated? Amused?

I supposed that was a good thing when you were paid to be professional. Emotions were everything in my profession—I had to constantly tap into them. But the last thing a person looked for in a police officer was someone who easily burst into tears or who laughed at inappropriate times.

Alistair held up his hand and began ticking people off. "First of all, there's my old assistant. I fired her last week."

"Is she here on the island?"

"No. She'll stay far away if she knows what she's doing. Then there's the woman I passed up to give the lead role to Joey instead."

"Does this woman have access to the script?" Chief Chambers asked.

"Only the first few scenes. Finally, my financial advisor and I parted ways a few days ago."

"Did he do anything illegal?"

"He annoyed me."

The chief stood, her expression still placid. "Okay then. I don't see where a crime has been committed here. But I will keep an eye on the situation. Please let me know if there are any new developments."

"This is a crime." Alistair rushed to his feet also. "It's a crime against creatives. The kind of crime that most people don't care about because stuff like this supposedly comes with the territory."

She offered a sympathetic glance. "I assure you that we do care. Speaking from the viewpoint of the law, there's nothing that I can do right now. If anything else occurs involving bodily harm or theft, please contact me. Otherwise you may need to contact a lawyer or a private investigator. As of now, this is more of a civil suit."

As she walked away, Alistair's gaze fell on Washington and me. "I'm going to get to the bottom of this. No one is going to ruin me. No one. You hear me?"

His words caused me to suck in a quick breath. Passion pervaded each syllable. There was more to the story than he was letting on, wasn't there? This could be the beginning of something really ugly.

"All right, time is money." Alistair clapped his hands in the air as he stepped out of the trailer.

I followed behind him and saw that a majority of the cast and crew had gathered outside his trailer, waiting for instructions. When I said majority, I meant all eight of us. We were working with a skeleton crew and only three actors in the entire film.

As soon as everyone saw Alistair, they scrambled to attention.

"Let's get back to work," Alistair continued. "Why are you all standing around?"

But before any of us could get in position, a sound echoed across the beach.

I turned to see an angry mob of pirates headed right toward us.

An angry mob of pirates? What in the world was going on here?

I didn't know, but I did know that things had just gotten a lot more interesting.

CHAPTER
THREE

"DID Alistair add pirates to this movie?" Washington whispered in my ear as we stood on the steps of Alistair's trailer watching everything play out.

My eyes were fixated on the scene in the distance. There were probably twenty people dressed as pirates, hooting and hollering like they'd just run aground.

Several raised swords in their hands. Fake swords? I could only assume. I saw at least one person with a hook on his hand, and a couple people held shovels.

The mob headed toward the lighthouse, oblivious to the camera crew.

How had they gotten past security? A guard was

stationed at the entrance to this area. My guess was that they'd run down the beach on the sandy shore, which was sometimes impassable because of the tide. I only knew that because someone had told me earlier.

I'd arrived in town last night, and I'd run into a couple of locals while eating dinner. They'd gone on and on about the history of this area. It had a pirate-filled past.

Washington's question floated back into my mind. *Did Alistair add pirates to the movie?*

"Not that I know of," I finally said. "But who knows what's been happening behind the scenes. Tomorrow the script might turn into *Shrek* meets *Avatar*."

I continued to watch as Alistair stormed toward the pirates. His arms flew in the air, reminding me of someone trying to scare off a flock of birds. If I had a camera right now, this could be YouTube gold.

On second thought, I was really glad I'd taken this job. This was pure entertainment. What more could I ask for?

"Just give me some popcorn and Milk Duds, and I'm set," I mumbled, still watching everything play out.

Washington glanced at my newly expanded rear

section. "I don't think you need any more Milk Duds."

I picked up a broken shell from the sand beneath me and tossed it at him. "Shut up."

"Did your mom ever tell you it's impolite to say shut up?"

"My mama was too busy being involved with an international crime ring."

Washington just gave me a look that clearly said he had no idea if I was joking or not. I wasn't. But my statement did shut him up about my sudden but not real weight gain.

"You know what the altered script means, don't you?" Washington whispered, changing the subject.

"That someone is messing with us?"

"It means there's someone on the *inside* who's messing with us."

I squinted and glanced at him. "What do you mean?"

"Only people on the set have a copy of that script. No way could anyone else be responsible."

I understood what he was saying but . . . "Why would someone do that?"

"That's a great question."

His statement lingered in my mind. I hated to think that there was someone on set we couldn't trust. But Washington's assessment made sense. That script was top secret.

Unease sloshed in my gut.

After a moment of watching the pirates surround Alistair, I decided that maybe someone should help him. His crew all stood near me, looking like they had no idea how to handle the situation. This scenario wasn't exactly listed in any of the Hollywood Survival Guide study materials.

I started toward him, already feeling the sun beginning to get to me. Summer had passed, but it was hot out here on this lonely stretch of the coast. The silicone bodysuit I wore probably weighed twenty pounds, and breathing had become so difficult I felt like Mandy Moore in the shark cage in *47 Meters Down*.

I could feel my breaths coming quickly. It was funny what wearing the outfit did to me mentally. I already felt more out of shape than I actually was.

Then again, walking across what was known as sugar sand was never easy, no matter what kind of shape I was in.

I charged toward the angry mob just in time to hear everyone talking like a pirate. I guess that shouldn't surprise me. They *were* all dressed that way. Alistair tried to talk some sense into them, but none of them seemed to want to hear it.

"Avaste, ye!" I yelled.

Everyone turned and looked at me.

"That means halt ye activity and listen up," I told Alistair. "I played a pirate in a movie once." I turned back to the crowd. "What are you swashbucklers doing here?"

"This is where the X marks the spot!" One of the pirates—one who looked a lot like Blackbeard—stopped and pointed to the ground beneath him.

"Ye looking for treasures?" I asked.

"Yes, we arrrr!"

I stifled a laugh. This was no time to be amused. "Sorry, there be no treasure around here."

"That's not what the map says," Blackbeard continued.

"What map?"

"The one left fer us at our campsite." Blackbeard held up what looked like an antique piece of parchment paper.

Before he could realize what I was doing, I snatched it from him and studied the pictures there before handing it back.

"I'm sorry to say, but this is a fake," I told him. "Take the wisdom of this old woman who's lived many a day on this unforgiving landscape. You were all used as pawns by an unseen enemy."

"An unseen enemy?" one of the pirates asked.

"That's right. One who likes to employ sirens and the kraken."

They all gasped.

"Like in *Pirates of the Caribbean*?" one of them asked.

"Precisely. This ground is haunted. I'd leave if I were you. Now go before there's keelhauling. Don't be scurvy dogs."

Everyone gasped again.

"Go," I repeated. "This is a closed area."

The group turned and, with deflated shoulders, began walking back in the direction they'd come. I had a feeling this wasn't over, though. Did some of them really think there was treasure here? And—it seemed like a longshot—but was this somehow connected with those script changes?

"Impressive," Alistair mumbled, turning back toward me.

"What can I say?" I tried to blow on my fingertips, but with my false teeth, I may have spit instead. "I am paid to be someone I'm not."

Which wasn't impressive. Or attractive. Or . . . anything else I wanted to be.

"I heard there was a pirate cosplay event in town," Alistair muttered. "I never thought they'd show up here."

"At least they're gone now."

Satisfied that I'd done my job, I turned to head back to the set. But as I did, I ran into a familiar figure—a figure who had just witnessed me in all of my Joey glory.

CHAPTER
FOUR

MY HEART RACED as my most favorite face ever came into focus. My embarrassment quickly turned into delight.

"Jackson! You're here! You're . . . early!" He wasn't supposed to arrive until later tonight.

My fiancé stiffened as I threw my arms around him. Concern ricocheted through me. Why was he reacting like this? We hadn't seen each other in three weeks. I'd expected . . . I don't know. Something more swoon-worthy, I supposed.

"Joey?" He squinted at me. Even in his confusion and bafflement, he was so handsome. Square face, scruffy beard, and short, light-brown hair.

As Jackson and I stood here on the windswept, barren stretch of land, I couldn't help but think we looked as if we could be filming our own movie . . .

only, it wasn't a romance. Maybe it was more like an offbeat horror flick.

Jackson still stared at me. I touched my face, my cheeks, my wrinkles. Despite the changes, I still looked like me, right?

"It's me."

Jackson continued to squint.

I hadn't been concerned about him seeing me like this, but suddenly I realized that maybe I should be concerned. Alistair's words echoed in my mind. *You look hideous.*

"Joey?" Jackson nearly gawked as he stared at me, still keeping me at arm's length.

Maybe I should have warned him . . . "I mean, I know I've added a few wrinkles . . ."

"I can't believe it's you." The questioning tone left his voice, and now he just sounded flabbergasted. "You look so . . . so . . . different."

"I'm a woman of many faces. An agent of intrigue. A chameleon."

Jackson stared at me, still looking perplexed.

I gave up and dropped my act. "Moving on—what are you doing here already? I thought you weren't coming until tonight."

I touched my triple chin, feeling more self-conscious than I wanted. I mean, when Captain

America saw Agent Peggy Carter after sixty-some years had passed, he hadn't been repulsed.

Then again, Agent Carter had aged gracefully, whereas I'd let myself go . . . kind of. I mean, I looked more like Nanny McPhee if she had a water retention problem.

"I was going to fix myself up for you," I continued. "Make myself presentable and all."

I tried to read the look in Jackson's eyes, but I couldn't get a feel on what he was thinking right now.

"I . . . I thought I'd surprise you."

"It looks like I'm the one who surprised you."

He said nothing and instead extended his arm, handing me a bouquet of sunflowers. "For you."

"They're beautiful. Thank you."

"Okay, people." Alistair appeared. Or had he been there the whole time? "We need to get back to work. Time is wasting away. We're going back to the real script."

The way Alistair said the word "real" made it sound like the rest of us were idiots for ever believing the revision had been legit.

"I have a seat just for you," I whispered to Jackson. I'd had a special director's chair made for him, complete with his name across the back. Actually, I'd had "Joey's Stud Muffin" written there, just to amuse myself. "I'd take time to introduce you but . . ."

"I understand. Do your thing. We'll have time to spend together later."

My heart warmed. I handed him the flowers back. "Hold these for me until I can put them in water."

"Of course."

Jackson was here, I mused. My Jackson. Now everything in my world felt right.

And it would stay that way—as long as no one tried to rewrite my life script like they'd done for this movie.

My day on the set had proven to be grueling. At certain times, the temperature had felt burning hot. At other times, a blustery wind took over and sand-blasted us. My suit and makeup were making me miserable, and Alistair was acting like a brat.

Because it took so much time for me to get suited up, we would be working long hours to complete this within our given timeframe. I'd known that when I signed up for this movie. But it was really hard for me to focus on work when I knew Jackson was so close. I just wanted to see him and spend time with him.

It had been three weeks since he'd come down to visit me in Filmington, North Carolina. Actually, the city was Wilmington, but locals had given the area the moniker. I thought the nickname was cute and appropriate since so many movies and TV shows were shot in the area.

The hardest part about my life right now was that I couldn't always be with Jackson. I was determined to make our lives blend, to make our relationship a priority. But we needed to work some things out first—starting with making our schedules mesh.

Finally, Alistair called it quits after many, many hours and uncountable retakes. I glanced at my phone and saw it was almost midnight. Jackson had made it through filming like a champ. I hadn't heard a word out of him. He'd just sat in his chair, watching everything and soaking it all in.

I made my way toward my trailer. Thankfully, lights had been set up in the area so the crew could see what they were doing. Otherwise, it would be pitch black out here.

As I looked toward Jackson, I spotted someone talking to him.

I tried to ignore the twinge of jealousy I felt, but it was there.

Eva Angel—who played my nemesis in this

movie—was smiling, twirling her blond hair, and batting her eyes at Jackson.

Jackson laughed back.

And . . . Eva held the sunflowers Jackson had given me.

The twinge of jealousy grew stronger. Didn't Jackson know he wasn't supposed to laugh with Eva? That the deeply insecure part of me hated to see him with women I considered more beautiful than me? Especially when I wore outfits like this while she looked already photoshopped for a magazine cover.

"Hello there," I called as I trudged through the sand toward them.

Both Jackson and Eva straightened as if my appearance surprised them. Jackson jumped to his feet and took my arm.

"Joey . . . Eva was just introducing herself."

I attempted to smile at her. Though we were only supposed to be enemies on the set, something about the woman rubbed me the wrong way.

Despite that, I decided to put on my big girl pants. I trusted Jackson. I really did. It was my own insecurities that I worried about.

I cleared my throat. "I'm glad you were able to meet. But since I couldn't do a proper introduction . . . Jackson, this is Eva. Eva, this is Jackson . . . my fiancé."

I might be insecure and attempting to act mature, but I wasn't stupid. I needed to leave no doubt in Eva's mind that Jackson was mine, all mine. I mentally clacked my fingers together and grinned like a psychotic villain plotting a devious plan.

Eva's gaze darkened. "You've got yourself quite a gal here, Jackson. And Joey, I'm sure it's good to find someone who can love you, warts and all." A thin laugh left her lips.

I let out a fake chuckle and tried not to end it with a sneer. Instead, I turned to Jackson. "I just need to get changed and then I'll be right out."

"Sounds good."

I extended my hand. "And I'll take my flowers."

Eva glanced at her hand, and her lips twitched. "Of course."

Back in my trailer, I stripped out of my costume so fast that I briefly considered switching careers and becoming a quick-change artist. That idea lasted about as long as it took me to put on a new outfit.

In less than fifteen minutes, I was back out to meet Jackson. I felt more like myself without all my new layers on—with my warts gone, my wig off, and my false teeth in a container being sanitized. Instead, I'd donned my favorite skinny jeans and a blue sweatshirt, and wore my hair pulled back into a ponytail.

Eva scampered off when she saw me, and I took Jackson's arm, happy to have her gone.

I'd come to realize there were toxic people in this world—people with no moral compass. You had to be cautious of those kinds, for your own protection. I'd learned that lesson the hard way.

Most of the crew had already left. I gripped my flashlight and looped my arm through Jackson's as we made our way to the small parking lot in the distance. The moon shone brightly overhead, but otherwise things were eerily quiet.

A security guard, Larry, would stay on the set this evening to make sure no one touched our things. I thought I caught sight of him sleeping in his car in the distance, which gave me total assurance that everything was safe under his watch.

Or not.

"I know you're probably tired," I told Jackson. "I'm sorry to keep you up so late."

"No apologies necessary." Jackson took my hand. "You remember the last time we were here in Lantern Beach?"

"Of course." How could I forget? I'd almost died. But the good news was, I had discovered my father. All in all, I had mixed feelings about this place, but no one could deny it was beautiful.

"It seems like a million years ago, doesn't it?"

"It really does." How long had it been? I tried to recall. Not even six months, if I remembered correctly.

We paused in the parking lot by Jackson's truck, and all I wanted to do was reach up and give him a proper kiss—I could do that now that my false teeth were out.

These were the things I never thought I would think to myself.

Before I could do anything, a footstep sounded beside us.

I looked over and saw a pirate standing there, with a dagger raised toward Jackson and me. All I could think was, shiver me timbers.

CHAPTER
FIVE

"YOU'VE GOT to help me. Someone wants me to walk the plank, mateys." The man stared at us, a crazy look in his eyes.

He'd stepped out of the woods wearing black trousers, a black waistcoat, and a pirate hat. Even in the dark, I could feel the man's nervous energy.

Jackson nudged me behind him, not looking frightened as much as annoyed.

Me? I was as nosy as a pig in front of a new batch of slop.

"Walk the plank? Like, literally?" I asked, unsure what was going on here.

At least the dagger appeared fake.

I squinted, trying to study the edges in the dark.

Most likely it was fake. If it were real, Jackson would be all bristly right now.

I squeezed Jackson's bicep. Nope, it definitely wasn't as hard as it could be.

"You know what they say?" The man showed his teeth, reminding me a little too much of a middle-aged Jack Sparrow with a dad bod. "Dead men tell no tales."

What in the world was this man talking about? Why was he still in character? I didn't know whether we should run for our lives or hear him out.

"This is all your fault," Jackson leaned toward me and muttered softly.

"My fault? Why?" I wasn't Batman. I hadn't sent a Joey-Signal, telling all the freaks in the area that I was here and, if they were distressed, they could find me.

"You're the one who insisted on talking to them like pirates earlier. Now he thinks you're one of them."

"I was trying to show a common bond so they would listen to me. It's a classic negotiation tactic—"

"Arrr!" The man lunged toward us, that crazy look still in his eyes.

Or was that eyeliner that made his eyes look like that?

"Could you just talk in plain speak?" I took a deep breath, wondering if I would regret my questions. "Please. Because as much as I love pig slop, I'm really tired right now."

"What?" Jackson muttered.

The man lowered his dagger and stared at me, recognition spreading through his gaze. "I thought it was you."

"Me?" I pointed to myself.

"Yes, you. Joey Darling. Actress extraordinaire. World-famous detective. Eye candy—"

"That's enough," Jackson murmured.

I could feel Jackson's eyes on me, staring at me as if saying, *I told you so.* I'd never seen this pirate before.

Unless . . . he was one of the pirates who stormed the set earlier. But, if so, that didn't count. I had nothing to do with that little invasion.

"I need me a detective," he said. "Before someone feeds me to the fishes."

"I'm not really a detective." If I had a penny for every time I had to say that one . . .

"I heard you were in town, and I knew it was fate that brought our paths together."

Jackson stepped forward, his patience obviously dead and buried at this point. "It's been a very long day. We really should go—"

"Someone really is trying to kill me. You're the only ones who can help."

I glanced at Jackson and saw him release a long breath before crossing his arms. He finally asked, "Why do you think someone is trying to kill you?"

"Because of this." The man reached into his pocket.

Jackson tensed beside me, as if preparing to go on the defensive. Waiting to see a gun. A knife.

Instead, the man pulled out . . . a piece of paper. In crude red letters were the words, "Heed my warning or you will die."

"I guess that explains where the notion that he might die came from," I murmured, leaning against Jackson's truck. "Although, I must say, the threat really could be more specific. Maybe this bad guy needs to work with a criminal coach who can help him refine his message a little more."

Jackson gave me a look that showed he clearly questioned my sanity.

Me too.

When he turned back to the pirate, his eyes took on a new light, as if he were fully engaging in detective mode. "Any idea who sent this or why?"

"I have no idea," the man said. "I'm just a poor pirate . . ."

"If you want our help, tell us who you are," Jackson growled. "Who you *really* are. If you give me a pirate name, I'm climbing into my truck and driving away."

The man's face transformed from dopey to halfway normal. "Gene Belching, but my friends call me Bucky."

"Belching?" I questioned. Was that a real last name?

"It's legit." He rolled his eyes. "Believe me, I've heard about it for my entire life."

"Where are you from, Mr. Belching?" Jackson asked.

"New Jersey."

"Do you take this threat seriously?" Jackson continued. "Is there any reason you can think of that someone would want you dead?"

"None. I'm a blue-collar worker. Single. Poor. You tell me why someone would want me dead."

"So this threat is just out of the blue?" I clarified. "There's been absolutely nothing leading up to this point?"

"That's correct," he said with a strongly affirmative nod.

I was no expert on these things, but I had to wonder if someone was just pranking him.

"Listen, maybe we can talk tomorrow." Jackson put his hand on my lower back. "It's late right now.

Why don't you give me your number, and I'll give you a call?"

"Fine." The man grunted and spouted out his number, waiting as Jackson typed it into his phone. "I'll look forward to hearing from you. Hopefully, I'll live long enough to do so."

Jackson and I stood in the lot after the man disappeared back into the woods. I had no idea where Bucky Belching was going or why he didn't simply walk up the lane as he departed. I might have called out and asked him, but I didn't.

Instead, silence fell.

I didn't think either Jackson or I knew exactly what to say after that conversation. The rest of the cast and crew appeared to be gone, and the security guard was probably asleep in his car still.

But this wasn't how I wanted to end my day and say goodnight to Jackson. I knew he'd gotten a room at an Airbnb, but I needed more time with him before we went our separate ways.

"Let me drive you home," Jackson said.

Nothing sounded better but . . . "I have to be back here tomorrow morning by five. If I leave my car here—"

"I'll drive you." He started toward the other side of his truck to open the door for me.

"Are you sure? It's early—"

"I'm positive. I came here to be with you. That's what I intend on doing—even if that means being up well before the sun."

My heart warmed. His words were music to my ears.

I'd anticipated talking to Jackson about us and the future as we headed down the road. But as soon as we climbed into his truck, all I could think about was that weird conversation with the wannabe pirate. It seemed like a shame not to address it.

Address it and move on. That's what we should do.

"Do you think that man was crazy?" I asked, pulling my seatbelt on.

"Probably."

"Do you think someone is trying to kill him?"

"The threatening note was a little obscure. This really is a matter for local police, though. Besides, you're going to be filming a movie. There's not much you can do. And I'm here to spend time with you, which means there's not much I can do."

"True."

"Anyone who hangs out at this hour and appears from nowhere strikes me as odd."

"Maybe he's scared."

"Maybe he's up to something."

As much as I tried not to think about the encounter as we drove to my house, of course I did. Not only was Bucky Belching's appearance weird, but so was the earlier swarm of pirates on the set.

And what about that treasure map? Why would someone create one of those? Was it to interrupt filming? Or was someone messing with the pirates?

Fifteen minutes later, Jackson and I pulled up to my place. He took my hand and said nothing as we paced to the front door.

"I know it's late, but I haven't seen you in weeks," I said. "Can you come in for a little while?"

"I'd love to."

We stepped inside my rental. I had told Alistair that a room at a local bed-and-breakfast would be plenty. But he'd insisted on getting me this fancy house. Considering his budget, I was surprised he'd picked this out for me.

Not long ago, I bought myself a beach house in Nags Head, a tourist town that was a hop, skip, and jump away—if one visualized the islands as leap pads. I absolutely adored the place with its wrap-around porches and salty breezes.

But this place where I was staying while here in Lantern Beach was more of a luxury. It had three floors, a swimming pool, and every amenity a person could want. And it was all mine for the next two weeks.

"Can I fix you some coffee?" I asked Jackson.

"I'd love some." He followed me into the kitchen and looked around. "Nice place."

"I know. I thought it was pretty nice myself. Too bad I won't be able to spend much time here." I poured some water and then began scooping grounds into the filter. The aromatic smell of bold roast with a hint of hazelnut drifted up to me.

Jackson lingered behind me, watching my every move. "Is that right? You have a grueling filming schedule, huh?"

"Yeah, something like that. As I told you before, we have only two weeks to complete this. We didn't get off to a great start." Memories of today's filming battered me, making me feel like I'd been in a fist fight.

"That's what I gathered."

After I started the coffee, I turned around and sucked in a breath when I realized Jackson was right there, only inches away from me—if that far.

I filled the gap between us. As I looked up into his gaze, I realized just how much I had missed Jackson. No, I took that back. I'd known without a doubt that I missed Jackson terribly. But, looking at him, I was just reminded of all the time that had passed since I'd last seen him.

I reached up and skimmed my hand along his jaw, feeling the scruff of his five o'clock shadow. It felt so good to be near him, to see his hazel-green eyes, and to smell his spicy aftershave.

On my tiptoes, I stretched up and planted a kiss on his lips. Man, I had missed doing that. I pretty much missed everything about our life together. I kept telling myself I would get used to the change, that our lives would eventually match up, but how much time would it take?

Finally, the coffeemaker stopped gurgling. And I'd been kissing Jackson that whole time without apology.

I poured Jackson a cup. I didn't need one. I was already wired.

"Don't you need to get some sleep?" Jackson studied my face. "I know you have a long day tomorrow and you want to be fresh."

"Are you kidding? The worse I look, the better it is for this role I'm playing. Bags under my eyes? Check. Coffee-stained teeth? Check. The haggard gaze of someone who's clearly overextended herself? Check."

Jackson chuckled. "This doesn't sound anything like the Joey Darling I know."

"Well, I've turned over a new leaf. It's a moldy, crumbling new leaf, but it's a new leaf."

Jackson chuckled again and pulled me into another hug. I'd missed that reaction. It was pure Jackson.

He had the ability to be tough, to be strong, and to set boundaries. He also left no doubt that he loved me immensely. Maybe—just maybe—deep down inside, I actually amused him.

And I loved that because I secretly craved making him laugh. I loved seeing that flash of humor in his eyes. My dad had always said I was a natural-born entertainer.

I took Jackson's hand and led him to the couch. I didn't care if I got any sleep tonight. I just wanted to talk to him, to hold his hand, and to catch up on the life we'd missed doing together the past few weeks.

Before I could dive into my questions about his job as a detective in the Outer Banks, he spoke up.

"So tell me about this movie," Jackson said. "It seems . . . I don't know . . . I'm no expert on Hollywood or the film business, but the script seems weird."

I told him about today's shenanigans, and he listened intently, grunting and nodding and grunting and nodding in all the right places.

"I guess I shouldn't be surprised," he said. "These things always seem to happen to you, don't they?"

"Yeah, I guess you could say they do. But having somebody send a new script out? That's just crazy. I've had a lot of weird things happen in my life but never that."

"Who do you think did it?"

"I have no idea. To be honest, I really don't know that many people on set. I mean, I've worked with a couple of them before. I've heard rumors about some of them, and I've read articles about others. But I don't know anyone well enough yet to be able to say who might do something like this."

"But you think it's someone on the inside?"

"Oh, yeah, I definitely think this has to be someone on the inside. The question is why? Why would someone do this? It makes no sense."

"Maybe somebody really does want to sabotage this movie," Jackson suggested.

"That is a possibility. But for someone to want to sabotage this movie, they're going to great lengths to do so. Why would they do that? Is this about Alistair? Does someone have that big of a grudge against him? Do they feel he wronged them? Or maybe they feel slighted and that he didn't give them a big enough role? I have no idea, but I think it's going to be interesting to see what happens next."

"I think it'll be interesting too," Jackson said. "Then again, things are always interesting when Joey Darling is involved."

I flashed a smile and batted my eyelashes. "Isn't that just the sweetest thing you've ever said to me?"

"You're one of a kind." Jackson quickly planted another kiss on my lips before leaning back.

He played with my hand, running his fingers in and out of mine while sitting incredibly close. I rested my head on his chest, wishing I could freeze this moment.

"So, some time we're going to need to talk about our wedding," he murmured.

I sat up straighter at the change of conversation. "Yes, we absolutely do. I am so ready to set a date and have this figured out and become Mrs. Jackson Sullivan."

"I know our schedules have been so crazy lately that we haven't really had the time we need."

I pulled out of his embrace and grabbed my cell phone. A moment later, my calendar showed on the screen. "All right. We're still thinking the spring, right?"

"That is what we discussed. I am thinking maybe the end of April, beginning of May. How does that look for your calendar?"

I scrolled down until I reached those dates. It was

still about six months from now. Some people would say that wasn't enough time to plan a wedding, but I wasn't looking for anything too big or fancy.

Jackson and I had both been married before. His marriage had ended when his wife died of breast cancer, and mine had ended with an abusive, narcissistic husband.

It wasn't the way either of us had seen our lives turning out. But reality was reality, and the past was the past. Now we were both ready to move forward.

I'd already done the big wedding in the limelight with the paparazzi and media following me when I married another movie star. Now I just wanted something simple, laid-back, and private. But mostly I just wanted anything I could get with Jackson.

"You said the end of April, beginning of May?" I stared at those dates on my calendar. In theory, they should work, but . . . "I'm supposed to be wrapping up filming of that other movie right about that same time. I'm afraid that filming might run over, and it's taking place in New Zealand, and I don't want that to happen and for things to have to be rearranged because of it."

His lip twitched.

Twitched? What did that mean? That was some kind of body language, I just couldn't remember what. Did it mean he was unhappy? Deep in thought? Constipated?

"Okay, then, how about the middle of May?" Jackson said. "It's still nice outside, and not too hot, not too cold."

"Kind of like April 25, where all you need is a light jacket."

Jackson gave me a look.

"*Miss Congeniality*? Haven't you seen it? The beauty pageant host asked her about the perfect date and—" I shook my head. "Never mind. Yes, I could schedule something around that time, except . . ."

"Except what?"

"I think I agreed to do a media blitz around that time for *A Useless Ending to a Hard-Fought Life*. Right now, it's scheduled to release in June, so that's going to be right about the time all of that happens."

"Okay, so looking at your calendar, what's open for you?

I stared at my schedule for the next . . . well, basically for the next year. Why was it that, after taking a little break from acting, I had jumped back into things with both feet?

I'd been afraid I wouldn't be able to get any roles after my ex-husband ran my name through the mud and started lots of vicious rumors about me. But, after a little sabbatical, not only had I gotten my role back as Raven Remington on *Relentless,* but the movie offers had also been pouring in.

I'd been trying to be choosy about what I picked to do. I could finally afford that luxury in my career. But I'd been getting some really good scripts that I thought could do some really good things for my acting resumé.

I looked up at Jackson and frowned. "My schedule is pretty booked, but we can totally schedule something in here. I don't know why this feels entirely more difficult than it has to be."

Jackson's gaze caught mine. "You're not changing your mind, are you?"

"Changing my mind?" My voice lilted with surprise. "Oh, no. It's nothing like that. I haven't changed my mind. I want to marry you more than millions of women want to meet Jason Momoa."

He chuckled. "Good to know."

"My schedule is going to be like the Titanic, and you're going to be the iceberg that wrecks it." I was on a roll with my analogies here.

"What?" Jackson asked.

"I just mean, let's find the two weeks we need, and make it happen." Maybe I was trying a little too hard and was a little overly excited about Jackson being here.

He raised his eyebrows. "Two weeks? Our wedding is a two-week affair?"

"Oh, no, not the wedding itself. But there's also the rehearsal, the bridal shower, and the bachelor party. The rest of the time we're totally going to be on our honeymoon."

He let out a murmur of approval. "I like that idea. Where are you thinking we should go?"

"I don't know. How about an island in the Caribbean?"

"I could handle an island in the Caribbean with you."

I couldn't help but smile at the idea of it. But we were still talking about something that was six months away. It seemed like forever. Not that Jackson wasn't worth the wait.

"All right, so let's think about a wedding in early May. I'll have to run these dates past my bridesmaids. And my dad—" I stopped myself as I said the words.

My dad? More than anything I wanted him to be there for the ceremony. But after an ugly turn of events, he was in the wind again. And so was my mom. It was a long, complicated story, but Mom was mixed up in some pretty bad stuff, and, as a result, Dad had gotten mixed up in some bad stuff too.

Here I thought she'd just run off to start a new life

away from Dad and me. In truth, she'd gotten involved with an international crime ring. Somehow my dad had found out about her association and gotten pulled into it, and now he was basically in witness protection somewhere.

I never thought I would say these things about my life. I was a simple girl from the mountains of Virginia. I hadn't intended on pursuing acting. But acting and Hollywood seemed to find me.

Sometimes I wondered if my life would have been better if I'd continued to work as a hair stylist and did community theater on the side. I mean, I loved what I did. Don't get me wrong. But acting had changed me. All the things I had vowed not to do and not to be . . . I'd become those things and done those things.

My marriage ending had been a wakeup call. Suddenly, all the mistakes I'd made became clear.

I had fled to the Outer Banks of North Carolina in order to find my father and to make things right in my life. That's when I had met Jackson. Though our relationship had a rocky start, once we realized we loved each other, there was no turning back. He'd become the Ricky to my Lucy.

The one thing that was certain was that my life today looked nothing like it had only two years ago. I like to think that I had grown up, that I had matured.

But then I looked at my calendar and saw how many things I'd said yes to, and I had to wonder if I was taking steps backward. I told myself I was stronger than Hollywood. I told myself I was stronger than the draw of fame and success.

I thought I was. I really did. But I had to be careful because pride did come before a fall. My dad had highlighted that in his old Bible—the one I kept. I liked to look through it and see the notes he'd scribbled in the margins. It reminded me of my childhood, of my past, of the things that were important in life.

I was about to look at my calendar again so I could reconfirm some of these dates when I heard a ding. I knew I shouldn't do it. But like a chocoholic being offered some pie with ganache, my fingers found themselves hitting a little email icon on my phone.

The screen changed, and I saw I had just gotten a new email. From Alistair.

As soon as I saw it, my back muscles clinched. An email? From Alistair? At this time of night?

With a curiosity that I couldn't seem to stop, I clicked on it. My eyes widened when I saw that it was an updated script. I showed it to Jackson, and he let out a grunt.

I couldn't wait to see what these changes were.

CHAPTER
SIX

"A NEW SCRIPT?" Jackson stared at me.

I nodded and read the email aloud. "I know we had some issues with a supposed script change today, but this really is the one and only Alistair King, and this really is a script change." I cleared my throat. "Please review these changes and be ready to go through this at filming tomorrow. I expect you to be at your best and to come prepared so we can make the most of our limited time together."

I halfway expected him to end the email with, "You imbeciles!"

It was just the way Alistair liked to talk to address things sometimes. I didn't say I liked it. But he was quite the character.

Jackson leaned closer, staring at my phone screen. "You think Alistair actually sent that?"

I stared at the words there and shrugged. "I have no idea. I mean the wording sounds like him—the one and only Alistair King," I said, my voice taking on an air of snobbery. "But after everything that happened today, I can't be so sure."

"Why don't you open the document and see what it says?"

I clicked on the link and opened the revised script. The pages were formatted and looked exactly like our normal scripts. This time, the opening scene was back to normal.

It had my character stepping into the lighthouse to keep my eye on the area and look for any signs of trouble. It was what Drusilla did every morning, a habit borne of her many years of being a spy.

"So far, this looks the same," I muttered. I skipped ahead, trying to find any changes. I stopped where we were supposed to begin filming in the morning. Eva would film her part as double agent Tabitha Tyndale.

Except, in this new script, she appeared for just a few minutes only to vanish and never to be seen again.

I told Jackson.

"Something really strange is going on here, Joey." Jackson squinted as he stared at my phone.

"I agree. I have no idea who might be behind this

or why he or she might've sent us a new script again. It's one thing if someone does this once as a joke or to mess with Alistair's head. But why do it again?"

"That's a great question."

A bad feeling remained in my stomach. I seemed to have a radar for these types of things. Trouble followed me. Was that what was happening now? Or was I reading too much into this?

"The good news is that no actual crime was committed," Jackson reminded me. "This appears to be harmless. Hopefully, it stays that way."

"Hopefully. I guess I will find out tomorrow when I go on the set."

I glanced at my watch and saw it was already three in the morning. Jackson and I had been talking since we got here.

There was no getting sleep for me tonight, especially now that my mind was racing.

Just as the thought entered my mind, my phone buzzed. I'd gotten a text message. My eyes went to the number—it was an unknown caller.

But the words felt all too familiar and threatening.

This film will be the death of you.

I took that cup of coffee after all as I tried to sort through my thoughts. Jackson and I were still on the couch, but our relaxed vibe from earlier had disappeared.

"Why in the world would someone send this to me?" I asked, staring at my phone screen.

Jackson frowned, and I could tell he wasn't happy with this turn of events. "Why does anyone ever send you stuff like this?"

Point taken. "Is it a threat? Or is someone just reminding me that I could have made a very poor choice when selecting *A Useless Ending to a Hard-Fought Life* as my next movie choice?"

"Your guess is as good as mine."

We sat there for a few minutes in silence. I sipped my coffee and let my thoughts churn between the script, this threat, and the earlier encounter with the pirate.

Were all of those things connected?

"Do you think this is connected to the Bucky Belching guy?"

"Do I think it's connected?" Jackson gave me a look that was answer enough—his lip twisted at one end, his head tilted, his eyes held a no-nonsense look. "I think he's a quack."

"But he did get that note saying that somebody wants to kill him."

"He was also dressed in pirate costume, and he speaks with a fake accent while carrying a toy dagger. And, actually, the note said, 'Heed my warning or you will die.'"

"It's kind of a weird threat." I shook my head. "Alistair said there's a cosplay pirate event in town."

"I talked to some people when I was on the ferry, and they were telling me about it. Apparently, it was a last-minute thing, but locals are getting a hoot out of seeing pirates walking around here on the island."

My thoughts continued to churn. "You really don't think this guy is in imminent danger?"

Jackson suppressed a sigh and rubbed my arms. "Honestly, I have no idea. And it's not my job right now to have any idea. I'll let Cassidy and the crew worry about that. The only reason I'm here is to have some time with you."

My heart warmed. But, as instantaneously as it happened, my thoughts turned to what he said.

"Cassidy?" Who was Cassidy?

"She's the police chief here in town," Jackson said. "I met her when I came here to help search for some fugitives."

That was right. I vaguely remembered that. "You mean, Chief Chambers."

"You met her?"

I nodded. "Alistair thought it was a crime that his script had been revised. He called the police."

Jackson let out a chuckle "Shouldn't surprise me."

"She seemed nice and unexpected. I love seeing women who aren't afraid of fighting the bad guys."

"She seems like a stand-up gal. This island is lucky to have her."

I let out a long breath and straightened. This conversation was getting us nowhere. And I was losing my focus. Whether I liked it or not, I seemed to be turning into Raven Remington.

"All right," I finally said with a new resolve. "So we are not going to worry about this pirate and his threatening note. We are going to let the local police worry about that. In the meantime, I am going to film my movie. I'm going to spend time with you. And we are going to nail down our wedding date."

Jackson grinned. "That sounds like the perfect week off with you."

I put my questions in the back of my mind. Kind of. I mean, I was thinking about the pirate. A little. Because that's just where my mind went.

But I'd told Jackson I was going to let this go. So I would. I would try, at least.

Besides, I was going to be busy filming. There wouldn't be any time to be nosy.

In theory, at least.

CHAPTER
SEVEN

JACKSON and I had talked almost all night. Of course, all night really wasn't that long when considering I had to be on set by five and I didn't get home until past midnight. But it had been nice to catch up and to relax.

By four a.m., Jackson and I had decided to make breakfast together, and we sat outside on the deck to enjoy some omelets and fruit. It was dark outside still, but the stars shone, and we had fun trying to pick out the planets. The weather couldn't have been nicer—a balmy sixty-two degrees.

Right at five, I showed up with Jackson on the set. We waved at Larry—he was awake now and staring at his phone—as we pulled in. After Jackson checked everything out, he dropped me off at Mindy's trailer so I could begin to get suited up.

I had to get here so early because it took two hours to get me made-up and into my costume. I could see how this was going to get old quickly.

Once Jackson felt the area was secure, he went to talk to Larry. He wanted to know if the security guard had seen anything suspicious.

This film will be the death of you.

Why in the world would someone send me that? It made no sense.

But what if they were right? What if this film didn't help my career but hurt it? What if I got a Razzie for it? Actors' careers had been ruined because of poor movie choices. Take Hallee Berry, for example. After *Catwoman*, her star power was never the same.

I cast those thoughts aside as I sat in the chair and stared at a bleary-eyed Mindy. She looked like she hadn't gotten much sleep last night either. She was a second-generation Filipino American. She often wore her dark hair in pigtails and hardly wore any makeup herself. She didn't need to—her skin looked perfect.

"Morning," she muttered.

"Morning." My thoughts continued to churn. What would today hold? What did that revised script mean? Should I have checked on Eva or was that totally irrational? After all, Washington's character had died in the previously revised script yet he was just fine in real life.

Jackson and I had tried to find the source of the email. But, with our limited skills, we were unable to trace it back to the true sender. Someone must have set up a dummy account using Alistair's email.

"I saw the article," Mindy finally muttered as she blended the makeup on my face. "Sorry you have to go through that."

"The article?" I questioned. I had no idea what she was talking about.

"It was in the *National Instigator* this morning."

I stared at Mindy. "I can't say that reading the tabloids is the first thing I do every morning."

She frowned and put down her makeup brush. "Oh, sorry. I thought for sure you'd set up a Google alert for yourself so you'd be in the know."

"What article, Mindy?" My anxiety started to rise.

She frowned again, looking almost sympathetic. "The one that called you a diva and said that while the rest of the cast and crew had to stay at a rundown bed and breakfast, you had it put in your contract to stay in a luxury home by yourself."

My bottom lip dropped open at her words. "Are you serious?"

She nodded. "Yeah, I just saw it. It's definitely there."

"I didn't insist on that house. Alistair is the one who insisted."

She shrugged. "I'm just telling you what I read."

"What else did it say?"

"That you exhibited diva-like behavior. A closed set. An unlimited supply of IZZEs."

Anger grew inside me. I should be used to stuff like this, but I wasn't. "Where in the world did this person get their information?"

"I have no idea. But it was there. I'm sorry, Joey."

My jaw stiffened. I was sorry too.

I sat silently for several minutes as Mindy continued to transform me into Drusilla Fairweather.

My thoughts turned over and then over some more.

Who would have leaked that false information to the press? The best false information had some grounding in the truth, which made it harder to refute. I was staying at a large house alone, and it did seem wasteful, especially on a movie with this low budget.

The script changes still loomed over me like a threatening storm in the distance.

Part of me had wanted to call Alistair last night

when I got the email. But I feared that would cause him to wake up on the wrong side of the bed. That would make today miserable for all of us. Besides, no real crime had been committed, and I'd stick with the original script when filming began. No harm, no foul, right?

I had decided to wait until Alistair arrived this morning, and then I would tell him about the changes. I felt confident he wasn't the one who sent the revision, despite the compelling email accompanying it that had sounded strangely like Alistair. But what I didn't know was why somebody was so intent on toying with him.

I was sure this was a joke. But it was a pretty extravagant joke when you considered all the trouble someone had to go through in order to get the script in digital form and alter it, set up the dummy email account, and then to send it out to all the principal players.

As Mindy applied the wrinkles around my face, she lowered her voice. "You really think this movie is going to be any good?"

I looked at Mindy in the mirror. "I really don't know. But Alistair helped me out when I was just starting, so I thought I would help him out now."

"I heard he's changed."

"What do you mean?" I asked the question,

though I knew the answer. Kind of. I could tell he wasn't the newbie I had first started working with. Now he was more high-strung, more arrogant, more demanding. I supposed success did have a way of changing people.

"Well, after he did the *Jungle People* and it won all the awards, I heard that he became like an entirely different person. He made some money, got divorced, and started treating people like they were beneath him. Not many people want to work with him anymore."

Now that Mindy mentioned it, I had heard some things about that. In fact, based on what Alistair had told the police chief yesterday, his favorite hobby was firing people. His assistant? Financial advisor? Who knew how many other enemies he had?

Maybe it was something worth looking into . . . or maybe this was much ado about nothing.

CHAPTER
EIGHT

MY THOUGHTS SHIFTED from Alistair back to the script—and the fact that someone had changed the story so that Eva vanished.

As I shimmied into the suit that transformed my body into an overweight seventy-year-old, I decided to get Mindy's thoughts on things around here. She'd worked with this crew enough to have some insight.

"So what about Eva?" I ventured, holding my breath and feeling like a corset was being tied behind me as Mindy zipped up my suit. "I had no idea she was going to be working on this movie."

Mindy rolled her eyes. "I know. No one did. No one likes to work with her. But I heard that she and Alistair were a thing."

I froze. "For real?"

"Apparently, their relationship is all under wraps.

I mean, there is a striking age difference. But Eva is his type, so it wouldn't surprise me. It's probably how she ended up getting this role."

Alistair was in his early fifties while Eva was in her early twenties. Striking age difference would be correct.

Mindy stepped back to observe me. I briefly glanced in the mirror and frowned. This was not a good look.

"I think you're so brave to dress up like this," Mindy said, a solemn expression on her face.

I wasn't sure if I would call it brave. Maybe I was just foolhardy.

I glanced at my watch. I was supposed to meet Alistair here in a minute. I had a lot to talk to him about, including the script and the article that had been released calling me a diva.

Alistair was in a tizzy this morning. I was pretty sure that he had gotten even less sleep than I had, which was pretty miraculous considering I'd gotten none. I was also pretty sure he'd drunk more coffee than I had because his actions were wired and his words came so fast he sounded like an auctioneer who'd just drunk a Red Bull.

I tried to grab a second with him, but he was too busy fussing at Brandon about the importance of natural light. As I waited for him to finish, I glanced around.

Whoever had sent the revised copy of the script had started the revisions at the very spot where we were slated to begin filming today.

Who on the set could be behind this?

My gaze scanned everyone.

Rick, the director of photography. He was in his mid-fifties, had a cross-shaped scar on his cheek, and acted a little cranky. But he knew what he was doing.

Brandon, the gaffer/grip. He did lights and gear and occasionally worked the camera. He was quiet, with long hair he pulled back into a man bun.

Sarah, the production assistant. Just out of college. Shy and mousy.

Mindy, who did hair and makeup. She was friendly and liked to gossip.

Sai, audio specialist. From India. Always wore ear pods and never talked to people.

Larry had been hired to do security. He'd come from Raleigh and had supposedly been a cop for a few years. Jackson hadn't seemed impressed.

Washington George was already out here also.

But not Eva.

My breath caught. Where was she? Surely, she

was just getting ready. That had to be it.

I waited patiently near the camera for Alistair to finish before raising my hand. "Excuse me, Alistair, but there's something I need to tell you."

He flinched when he saw me, as if still not used to my new appearance—the appearance that he had written into this script.

"What is it, beautiful?" His words contained a hint of sarcasm.

I repressed the dirty look I wanted to give him. "I thought you should know that I got a new script early this morning."

He froze. "You what?"

"It's true. I got an updated script this morning. Eva's character goes missing in this version."

He glanced around. "Well, has anyone seen Eva?"

"I did," Rick volunteered. "She went into the honeywagon a few minutes ago and asked me to tell you she'd be late. Said something about needing to talk to her therapist a moment, but that she'd be right out."

In Hollywood, everyone had a therapist. It was as common as normal people having a dentist or mailman. That was a good thing—we all needed help with our mental health at times. Better to find it with a listening ear than with the bottle.

"Mystery solved. Eva is fine. Now, back to other

matters at hand." Alistair threw his hands in the air. "Why would somebody do this to me?"

No one said anything.

He shook his head one more time before his gaze became focused again. "It's time to get started. Is everyone ready?"

I knew that I was ready to get this over with, for sure.

"All right, everybody in place." Alistair clapped his hands in the air, reminding me of a flamenco dancer.

The crew scrambled to get to where they were going, and I took my place by the lighthouse. Today's scene actually did start here. Rick would get a shot of me outside the lighthouse, and then the scene would cut. I'd climb to the top and more shots would be filmed there.

Just as soon as Alistair called action, I grabbed the handle of the door and stepped inside. When I did, I let out a bloodcurdling scream.

Yesterday, I had seen Washington George lying on the floor surrounded by blood.

Today, Bucky Belching lay there. In his pirate garb. Fake dagger at his side.

But I had a strange feeling this was not fake.

The man looked honestly dead.

Just like the note had threatened.

CHAPTER
NINE

I SEEMED to go comatose as I stared at the body in front of me. Before I realized what was happening, Jackson appeared. He grabbed my arm before glancing down. He didn't have to feel for a pulse. Bucky was clearly and inarguably dead.

"Everyone, stay back," Jackson barked, suddenly in charge of this scene.

He pulled me away from the lighthouse and onto the sandy ground below. As he put an arm around me, he pulled out his cell phone and muttered something into it. Most likely, he was calling the police.

When he put his phone away, he pulled me into a hug. "Cassidy is on her way."

In the background, I could hear Alistair clucking around like a chicken. Or a flamenco dancer. Or someone else who liked to move a lot and make a lot of noise.

He kept saying something about time being money. I'd thought he'd be more concerned about the dead man than he was about his film, but he'd proven me wrong.

Something about that realization did not sit well with me.

But the fact remained that I'd already signed a contract to do this movie and to work with Alistair. Things seemed to be going downhill fast.

This film will be the death of you.

As I remembered the stark words on my phone, my heart rate quickened. What if that wasn't an empty threat? But why in the world would someone target me? I hadn't been in town long enough to upset anyone yet.

"Are you okay?" Jackson murmured.

"I guess. But the threat that someone sent Bucky Belching was real, Jackson," I whispered. "We were too late. Maybe we should've done something sooner to help."

He rubbed my arm as his gaze scanned everyone around us. He was doing what cops were programmed to do—watch over everybody and everything for any signs of trouble. "We couldn't have known. Besides, we were going to turn it over to law enforcement today."

"I know, but I can't get that man's image out of my mind. Why would someone do this? And whoever is behind this . . . are they somehow associated with this movie? I mean, otherwise, how would they know about that scene yesterday? How would they know that Washington George had been lying there? The only way it's possible is if the killer was on set."

One look at Jackson's face, and I knew he was thinking the same thing. Whoever was behind this was close. That left me feeling even more unsettled.

A few minutes later, Chief Chambers showed up along with two other officers. Her eyes lit when she spotted Jackson, and she strode toward him.

"Detective Sullivan," she said. "I didn't expect to see you here again."

He extended his arm and offered a hearty handshake. "When I heard Joey would be filming here, I knew I had to pay the island another visit."

"I wish you were here just to enjoy yourself, but it appears we have another crime on our hands." Her gaze wandered over to the lighthouse, and she frowned.

"Yes, it does." Jackson's jaw tightened.

We filled her in on what had happened. Alistair

joined us for a few minutes until the chief stepped away to see our victim.

Like a good girl, I waited outside. But my mind raced. I wanted to know what she saw, what she had discovered, and basically everything that was going on.

Did I deserve to know anything? No.

Would my nosiness be welcome? No.

But were my crime-solving skills to be admired? Also no.

There was a part of me that liked to find answers. I never said I was good at it, but there was something incredibly satisfying about helping people. About giving them the satisfaction of having answers. Having closure.

Maybe I knew that because of what happened with my own family. Having answers could be the start of a lot of healing. Knowing that I'd done something to help people? It was a good feeling.

Finally, Cassidy stepped out. I expected her to talk to Alistair again or maybe even Jackson. Instead, her eyes went to mine, and she started toward me, something in her hands.

"Joey," she started. "Did you know this man?"

I told her about my brief encounter with him the night before then asked, "Why? What's going on?"

"There was a piece of paper in his shirt pocket,"

she explained. "On the front, it said, 'Give to Joey Darling.'"

My breath caught, and Jackson moved closer, his expression darkening. What sense did that make? None. Unless this was about Bucky wanting to hire me.

"What else did it say?" Jackson asked.

"It's some kind of weird code."

I glanced at the number sequence.

17, 5, 12.

51, 2, 8.

4, 13, 2.

They went on and on, a whole list of them—probably thirty lines all together.

"Do you have any idea what these numbers mean?" Chief Chambers's inquisitive gaze latched onto mine.

I stared at the list, waiting for something to click. It didn't. I shook my head. "I have no idea."

But suddenly my stay in Lantern Beach was looking a lot more dangerous and more exciting than any film I'd ever shot.

Several minutes later, Alistair, Jackson, and I gathered in the production trailer and stood over the note with Chief Chambers. The medical examiner was on his way, and local police officers guarded the scene and documented any possible evidence.

The more I stared at the numbers, the less sense they made. All I could think about was the code-breakers from World War II. Maybe it was because I'd just seen *The Imitation Game.*

"Could it be some kind of locker combination?" Alistair asked. "Or maybe several locker combinations?"

"I suppose that's a possibility." Chief Chambers's eyes narrowed in thought. "But there aren't many lockers here on Lantern Beach. There are no gyms or self-storage facilities. I'm not sure that makes the most sense. My gut is telling me this might be something else."

"Maybe it's coordinates," I suggested. "Isn't that what it always is on TV?"

Alistair perked. "Yes, I had that in one of my movies one time. Coordinates. That must be what it is. Maybe it goes back to that buried treasure those pirates mentioned yesterday."

We filled Cassidy in on the pirates' visit.

Cassidy shook her head again, slowly this time as if she didn't want to offend anybody. "Nothing about these numbers strike me as coordinates. Besides, why would Joey's name be on that?"

Good point.

"Okay," I suggested, another idea hitting me. "What if this is some kind of secret code, and I have to interpret it in order to get the real message? I mean, this guy was a pirate, right? Maybe this is some kind of secret pirate speak."

Jackson nodded. "That's actually not a bad idea."

"I think I will question some of his fellow cosplay pirates who are in town," the chief said. "Maybe they'll know what this means."

"Any idea how he died?" I asked.

"It appears he fell from the spiral staircase leading up inside the lighthouse."

"I'm sorry to hear that." Alistair straightened and turned to the chief. "So what does this mean for filming?"

"Right now this means that this area is a crime scene. You definitely cannot film here in the lighthouse until we have all the evidence collected and documented."

"And how long might that be?" Alistair asked, his cheek twitching.

"We're looking at several hours," Cassidy said. "We're treating this as a potential murder. We have a possible killer loose on this island, and I intend on taking that very seriously."

"What about the filming I'm supposed to be

doing on the beach?" Alistair asked, something akin to panic fluttering in his gaze. "Could we go ahead and do that?"

"Not right now," the chief said. "I'm going to need this whole area cleared. We need to look for footprints, and we need to search the surrounding area as well. I can't risk having it tampered with by your crew."

Alistair's cheeks reddened. "You're costing me a lot of money, you know."

"I'm sorry, sir." Chief Chambers stepped toward the door. "But this takes precedence over your filming. I know you worked out a deal with the mayor to use this area. I'm sure he will do everything he can to make things square with you. But, right now, this scene is mine, and I'm yelling cut."

I had to resist a smile. I already liked this lady. But when I glanced at Alistair, I could tell he didn't share that sentiment. His cheeks remained red, and I could see him mentally counting how much cash he was losing by this delay in the production.

"Fine. Have it your way. I'm going to call a quick meeting of my cast and crew and then we will be out of your way."

"I will need to talk to people here on this set first."

Alistair's gaze swung toward Chief Chambers.

"Do you think somebody affiliated with this movie might possibly be involved?"

"Think about it," she said. "That makes the most sense. Your guys are the ones who have access to this area and to the script. Rest assured, we'll be fully investigating every aspect and every possible suspect. So please have your cast and crew stick around until I dismiss them individually."

Alistair's gaze narrowed again, but he said nothing. After a moment, he took a step back and nodded, as if resigned to do what he had to do. "Okay, they're all yours."

CHAPTER
TEN

THREE HOURS LATER, I was dismissed from the set. However, I was not able to take off my costume—only my false teeth. It would've taken too long for me to put everything back on. Just in case we were able to resume filming a little later, I needed to keep my look intact.

That meant I was free to roam the town with Jackson, but I was going to look like Drusilla Fairweather while doing so. It also meant it would be a lot harder to go to the bathroom if I needed to.

I had to admit I felt self-conscious when I climbed into Jackson's truck with wrinkles I hadn't earned, bags I could go on a shopping spree with, hair so thin my scalp needed extra layers to stay warm, and three chins I'd named Moe, Larry, and Curly. Curly was the one with the hairy wart.

That wasn't to say the people who look like this weren't attractive. But it was to say that right now I wasn't comfortable in my "own" skin.

Jackson looked at me after he cranked the engine. "Okay, so what now? Do you want to go back to your place?"

"I was actually hoping to get a bite to eat." Had I just said those words? That meant that not only was I leaving the set in my costume, but I was going to be going out in public like this. Did I really want to do that?

"You're okay with people seeing you as Drusilla?" Jackson asked. "You know how people are. If they see you, they might take pictures, and then those pictures might turn up in the tabloids and then . . . I mean, I'm fine with whatever you want, but I just want to double-check that we're on the same page."

"People won't actually know that I'm Drusilla. They'll see me and think I'm an older woman enjoying the area. I'm pretty confident that no one is going to recognize me as Joey Darling beneath this costume. I mean, you almost didn't recognize me like this."

"I can't argue with that, but I'm okay with it if you're okay with it. I just want you to know what the consequences might be."

"I am fine with it. I am Joey Darling, despite my size, despite my appearance, and despite all these new features I have that I did not have before."

That was right. Mindy had said I was brave. So I would be brave now. I would go and get a bite to eat in public while wearing this getup. In fact, maybe it would be kind of a nice social experiment. I would see whether I was treated differently if I looked differently.

Besides, if this was the bravest thing I ever did, then I really was spoiled.

"If you're sure." Jackson put his truck into Reverse.

"I heard about this restaurant in town called The Crazy Chefette. How about if we try that? I hear they have some awesome grilled cheese and peach sandwiches."

Jackson stole a glance at me. "I thought you weren't eating carbs?"

"At this point, it's not really going to make a difference." I rubbed my fake belly.

We drove along the road, the landscape beautiful around us. There were sand dunes on one side and marsh grasses on the other as we left the area around the lighthouse.

I'd been living in the Outer Banks for a while, so I should be used to this kind of beauty. I saw it all the time. But something about seeing it right now refreshed my soul.

The area reminded me that I was just a small part of a bigger picture. It reminded me that life wasn't all about me. And that was a good reminder to have sometimes, especially as an actress where life did go through periods where everything was about me.

But that was the old Joey Darling. I was trying to break out of those habits and mindsets. Still, I knew that it was easy to slip back into old ways.

I wanted to wait until Jackson and I were at the restaurant before bringing up anything pertaining to this case. After we ordered, I glanced around at all the interesting people here.

A group at the counter area laughed in a jolly manner. They appeared to be older men, mostly retired, and if I had to guess they probably came every day, doing this exact same thing.

At another table there were what appeared to be a bunch of surfers wearing wetsuits. On the other side of the restaurant, I saw several families probably here on vacation.

If I didn't live in Nags Head, I might have to consider this place. Lantern Beach had a great charm to it—even if I had almost died here while searching for my father and being stuck during a storm.

Jackson and I got our food, and I took a bite. The

grilled cheese and peach combination was actually amazing, as were the homemade potato chips.

After we'd eaten a few minutes without speaking, I broached the subject I knew was on both of our minds.

"Okay, Jackson, I know you're just on vacation and here to enjoy yourself. But that pirate, Bucky Belching? He was murdered. In the lighthouse. What do you think is going on?"

Jackson shrugged. "I have no idea, but I am sure that Chief Chambers will get to the bottom of all of this."

I frowned. I had to admit—I wanted more than he was willing to give right now.

Jackson let out a sigh and shifted. "Bucky Belching—or Gene Belching, I should say—wasn't that man's real name."

My eyes widened. "What? How do you know that?"

"Because I looked into him."

My eyes widened even more. "You did? Why?"

"Professional curiosity, I suppose."

I loved it when he got professionally curious. "Did you find out his real name?"

"Not yet. But, Joey, this doesn't mean you should get involved. You're not going to, right?"

"Of course not. Not by the hair of my chinny-chin-chin." I grinned and pointed to my newly added wart. "And check this out. I actually do have hair on my chinny-chin-chin."

Jackson stared at me a moment until finally a deep chuckle emerged, and he shook his head. "Joey, Joey, Joey . . ."

And suddenly, everything felt normal.

I kept chewing on Jackson's words.

Bucky Belching had used a fake name. Why? He'd sounded so believable. Talked about how he'd taken flak for his last name his whole life. Said he was a nobody from Jersey.

Had he come to the island with a hidden agenda?

Now that he was dead, it might be harder to figure out.

The truth was, every time I closed my eyes, I could see that man lying on the lighthouse floor.

Dead bodies were just not something I would ever get used to. I was sorry to say that I had seen more than my fair share of them. I'd learned that it was one thing to see a fake dead body like I did on sets. And it was an entirely different story to know that there had once been an actual life inside the now unmoving body.

"So . . ." I started, knowing there were some things I needed to talk to Jackson about—things other than Bucky. "Did you see the article today?"

He frowned and took a sip of his lemonade. "I did. I actually set up a Google alert for you. Just to stay on top of things."

"That's just about the sweetest thing that anyone —stalkers excluded—has ever done for me."

"Thanks . . . maybe. Anyway, I'm sorry, Joey. I know you hate stuff like that. And you're not a diva."

"I just can't figure out how that information was leaked."

"How about your super-stalker fan club?"

"I haven't heard from them in weeks."

"That doesn't mean they're not responsible."

"No, I suppose it doesn't." I frowned.

I tried to think of something else to talk about. I knew there were plenty of other things that Jackson and I could chat about. But my mind kept going blank. I kept running through those numbers and the fact that my name had been left on that note.

How could Jackson not want to talk about that? This was the biggest thing that happened since . . . since I found a dead body in my new house this past summer.

Why did these things always happen to me?

At that moment, two women in their early twenties walked past our booth. They squinted as they looked at me. It was almost like they recognized me but didn't really recognize me.

"That's so sweet," one of them whispered loud enough for me to hear. "Her grandson took her out to lunch."

I wanted to scowl. I really did.

But that only confirmed to me that Mindy had done a great job with this costume. Maybe I would actually like this. I could go out in public, and nobody would assume I was a detective that I actually wasn't.

That did it. No longer would I disguise myself in old hats and oversized sunglasses. From now on, I was going to let Mindy disguise me.

This film will be the death of you.

The words echoed in my head, followed by snippets from the article in the *National Instigator*. Someone here was keeping an eye on me.

At that thought, I glanced around again. Why did I feel like someone was watching me? Was it just paranoia?

I didn't know.

"What's wrong?" Jackson asked.

I shivered. "I don't know. It's just a feeling, I suppose. A feeling that something isn't right."

As soon as I said the words, my phone buzzed. It was another text message.

I'm watching you.

I glanced around again. The question was who. Who was watching me?

CHAPTER
ELEVEN

WHEN JACKSON EXCUSED himself to use the bathroom, one of the older, retired-looking men wandered over to me and paused by my booth.

"You must be Joey Darling," he said. The man was thin and wiry, with white hair and a matching beard and mustache. His eyes glimmered with intelligence and maybe even mischief.

"You recognized me?" I said, feeling halfway impressed.

"I was the police chief in town for about thirty years so I'd like to think I have decent skills of observation." He extended his hand. "I am Mac MacArthur by the way. Former police chief and current mayor."

"I'm Joey Darling. It's great to be here."

He shifted, his hand going to his hip. "You're the

talk of the town. Everyone's really excited that you're here and that you're filming your movie. We feel like Lantern Beach is a great town, and it deserves all the attention that it can get. Of course, we usually want the positive attention and not the negative."

"I guess you heard about what happened this morning." I frowned as I remembered the dead body.

"I chatted with Cassidy—Chief Chambers—and she informed me. I know that must've been quite shocking for you."

"Yeah, shocking is an understatement, but unfortunately this isn't my first rodeo."

"Funny that you say that," he said. "I actually read a couple articles on you before you came. Just trying to do my research and everything. I thought it was very interesting some of the crimes that you've solved in the past."

I shrugged. "I never really mean to. I just kind of stumble into these things. I can't help myself."

A grin spread across his face. "I think it's great. As long as you're safe, of course. I would never encourage civilians to get involved with these matters. But I have to say it makes for a great magazine story and *Dateline* special."

"It's like I always say, My successes are only because of my failures." My thoughts shifted. "Hey, maybe you can answer something for me. These pirates who are in town right now. What are they here for?"

"They're doing a pirate cosplay gathering, for lack of a better word. They're staying at a campground and having their 'gathering' at a local beach so they can reenact some pirate scenes from our town's history."

That made sense. "Is this an annual thing?"

"No, it was pretty last minute, actually. You should go watch them sometime. Most of their activities are taking place near the day use area by the lighthouse. There's a little campground beside it."

That was probably how they accidentally stormed onto the set.

"I guess you heard they accidentally wandered onto our set yesterday?"

"I did get a phone call about that."

"From Alistair?"

Mac grinned. "Yes, from Alistair. That was fine, though. I like to stay on top of what's going on here in town. I may be mayor, but the other part of me will always be this town's overseer."

"I guess every town needs an overseer. They're lucky to have you here in Lantern Beach."

He took a step back as Jackson joined us at the table. The two of them introduced themselves and discovered they'd actually met before when Jackson had worked a case here.

After we paid our bill and we were ready to leave, Jackson asked me where I wanted to go.

I knew I shouldn't. I really did. But I just couldn't help myself.

"I heard about this great recreational area near the day use area. It's not far from the lighthouse. Would you mind if we stop by there?"

I paused on the sandy beach and resisted a smile. Instead, I tried to utilize my acting abilities and show that my intentions in coming here were innocent.

I knew I would have to come clean before too long, though.

Jackson turned to me as we stood at the edge of the parking lot, looking at the beach in the distance where a skull-and-crossbones flag had been set up. "So. Pirates. Who would've thunk?"

"I know! They're here, of all places."

Jackson gave me a knowing look.

I didn't have to admit to anything. He knew me well enough to know I'd come here on purpose.

"So, what exactly did you want to do here, Joey?"

Jackson crossed his arms and stared at the beach in the distance.

"I don't know. I just thought the area was beautiful, so I thought we should stop by . . . and, I mean, I just wanted to get a better feel for these guys. Somebody *was* trying to kill Bucky Belching—or whatever his real name is."

"Correct."

"And I know there's a good chance that someone who's working on the set of this new movie is guilty. But there's also a good chance it could be one of these pirates. I really don't understand how the whole cosplay thing works. I think it's kind of weird. But I'm an actor, so some people think I'm weird. I pretty much have no room to talk."

"So we're just here to watch?" Jackson stared at me, and I knew he would catch me if I gave any hints that I wasn't being forthcoming.

"That's right, we're just here to watch. What else is there to do? I mean, except enjoy the beautiful view."

I turned my attention back toward the sandy beach. About twenty pirates went after each other, sword fighting and falling to the ground with fake injuries. It looked like a swashbuckling good time. Seagulls swarmed overhead, also seeming to enjoy the show.

As we stood on the edge of the sand, one of the pirates approached us. He wore the typical pirate garb and held a sword in his hand that he seemed to be using as a walking stick.

His squinty gaze remained on me as he got closer. "Ahoy, mateys. Didn't I see ye both yesterday on the set of that movie?"

"Maybe," I said. "You were one of the pirates who wandered down to the scene as we were filming, weren't you?"

"Yeah, I was." His expression changed, and he dropped his accent. "Sorry about that. I'm Lou, by the way. Lou Williams. Unfortunately, I was just killed in battle, and now I don't know what to do with myself."

"I'm sorry to hear that. It looks like you guys are having fun out here." I nodded toward the rest of the gang.

He shrugged. "We are, but we also heard about Bucky. We knew he wouldn't want this event to be canceled on his behalf, but I still can't believe it. None of us can."

"So you knew Bucky?" Jackson asked.

"Yes, we all did. The cosplay community, when it comes to pirates, is pretty small. We all know each other. This is one of our bigger get-togethers, but we have local get-togethers all the time and we talk online. Bucky was a very outspoken member of our community."

"Outspoken member? What do you mean?" I had to wonder if being outspoken was a good or a bad thing. It could mean Bucky had ruffled feathers.

"Oh, I just mean that Bucky loved this stuff. He fully embraced the pirate life. Most of us have regular jobs, and some of us even have families. We just do this on the side for fun. But Bucky—he really wanted to be a pirate."

"What do you mean?" I asked again. I didn't want to assume anything here.

"I mean, not like the evil kind of pirates from days past. But Bucky wanted to live like a pirate. He wanted to dress like a pirate. Eat like a pirate. He wanted to live on a pirate ship—a houseboat, actually. He even bought a parrot. He was totally into this kind of thing."

"He said he had a blue-collar job," I said. "Do you know what he did for a living?"

"He didn't say, but he was obviously making money somehow. He was always on the phone. He liked to do some photography for fun. He especially liked sunsets, he said."

"Do you know what his real name is?" I asked.

"I have no idea. Never asked. Didn't seem important."

"Did he have any enemies?" Jackson asked.

I looked at him from the corner of my eye. He couldn't resist, could he? Jackson would never admit it, but he was curious about what had happened.

I also knew he had to be careful not to step on Chief Chambers's toes. This was her territory, and I knew Jackson did not want to do anything that would interfere or make her feel uncomfortable. But I figured we were just having a conversation. That couldn't be but so bad, right?

"Did he have enemies?" Lou repeated. "I mean, sure we've all had our enemies. We have two competing crews here at our gathering this weekend. Pirates are very territorial, you see. We do lots of live-action role play and fighting."

"Did anything ever go beyond the cosplay fighting?" Jackson asked. "I know it's not supposed to be real, but certainly real life interferes sometimes."

"Yeah, I guess." Lou paused and glanced around. Then he stepped closer. "There is this one guy I saw Bucky arguing with last night."

I perked up. Maybe this was a lead. Not that I needed a lead. Because I wasn't getting involved. But I still wanted to know.

Before I could stop myself, I asked, "Who? What happened?"

"I'm not really sure of the details. I thought I

might ask Bucky this morning but . . . I mean, as you know, it's a little bit too late now. But I saw him fussing with Corky Keelhauler."

"Corky Keelhauler? Who's Corky Keelhauler?" And where did they come up with these names? Bucky Belching? Corky Keelhauler? Who was next—Polly Swashbuckler?"

"Corky is the captain of the pirate ship *Anger of the Seize*. I couldn't tell what he and Bucky were saying, but it looked pretty heated."

"Do you remember any more details?" Jackson asked.

"Most of us are staying at a campground here in town. I was out for a late-night walk when I saw the argument. The two of them were standing over by the trees. Their hands were flying in the air, and I could tell that they weren't happy. The only thing I heard was something about shooting or being shot. I assumed it was all pirate-speak stuff."

"Do you know any of the history between the two?" Jackson asked.

"No, not really. I try to stay out of things like that. In fact, I think I'm already saying too much." As if uncomfortable, Lou glanced around.

"We'll be discrete," I told him. "Thanks for sharing. I just have one more question."

Lou glanced around again. "What's that?"

"Where did you guys get that pirate map yesterday?"

"From Bucky, of course." Lou took a step away. "Now, I've got to go. I hope that the authorities are able to find the person who did this to Bucky—because I don't believe this was an accident. He was a good guy. He didn't deserve this."

He took a step away and paused.

"And, by the way," he said. "I think it's great to see a grandmother and grandson out together bonding like this."

I narrowed my eyes in a scowl.

As he left, Jackson glanced at me, a smirk on his face.

"Not a word," I warned.

He crossed his arms. "You're not going to be able to leave this alone, are you?"

I was about to answer when my phone buzzed. I looked down. It was a text from Alistair.

He wanted all of us back on set.

Now.

"Death to the one who seeks to oppress us and benefit only himself!" someone yelled in the distance.

It was one of the pirates. But his words stayed with me.

Generally, people killed because of betrayal,

vengeance, or to eliminate a threat. Which one of those fit Bucky's death?

If I could figure that out, maybe I could figure out who killed him.

Maybe me and my grandson Jackson could.

CHAPTER
TWELVE

"CRAZY EVERYTHING THAT HAPPENED, HUH?" Mindy powdered my nose as I awaited my turn in front of the camera. We'd apparently been cleared to use part of the beach again. "Crazy and disturbing."

"Definitely," I agreed. "Too many things are going wrong here."

"You can say that again." Sarah joined us, hugging a clipboard to her chest and wearing a frown. "I can't afford for filming to be shut down."

"Why do you say that?"

"My pay here barely covers my student loans."

"I'm sorry to hear that."

She shrugged. "I hope my cashflow will get better as I become more experienced."

In a few minutes, we'd begin filming again. I

knew Alistair had to be relieved that he would be able to accomplish something today, given our tight schedule.

As we geared up to begin production, I glanced at Jackson from my spot near the ocean and frowned. I was so thrilled he had come to see me and that I could spend time with him. But I hated the fact that I couldn't *really* spend time with him.

Mostly Jackson would be sitting in a chair behind the cameras, watching everything that happened while silently proclaiming to be my Stud Muffin. I loved him even more for being willing to sit around, bored to tears, just so he could be with me.

As I watched, Eva approached Jackson wearing a low-cut shirt and tight jeans. I must have scowled as I watched them.

"I wouldn't worry about her," Sarah whispered, following my gaze. "She only likes people who can advance her career."

Comforting . . . maybe. But there was something about the woman that made me not trust her. I tried to put it out of my mind and gear myself up for filming.

As I continued watching everyone around me, I saw Washington emerge from his trailer. He crumpled as he trudged across the sand.

"What's going on with Washington?" I asked, my

gaze following him. "He looks like he got bad news or something."

"Rumor has it he has a drinking problem," Sarah whispered.

"Really?" I stored that information in the back of my mind.

Alistair called, "Action," and Washington began reciting his lines. He had two pages of dialogue where he talked on the phone to someone unseen.

As the crew focused on him, I scanned everyone around me. I remembered what Cassidy said about someone who was a part of this cast or crew being responsible for Bucky's death—if it had been malicious.

While I still held the belief it could be a pirate, I also understood that Bucky's death mimicked the scene from yesterday's fake script.

Could someone I worked with be a killer? I repressed a shudder.

I didn't want to think that anyone I knew and trusted could be responsible. Then again, how many of these people did I really know?

I had worked with Alistair before. I had met Eva twice. I had been briefly introduced to Washington at a press event. But, mostly, all these people were new to me.

I felt a certain level of comradery with them

because we were all working on this film together. But it didn't mean they could all be trusted.

I knew that better than anybody. This was a cutthroat business. People whom you thought were friends weren't necessarily your friends. People in my line of business liked to look out for themselves.

Washington George? I didn't know a lot about the man. But Sarah said he turned into a different person when he drank, that he had a tendency to fly off the handle.

Mindy? Right now, she stood by so she could powder our noses when needed. The girl seemed too sweet to do anything nefarious.

My gaze went back to Alistair again.

Alistair . . . he had a large personality, a self-centered disposition, and he was known for his emotional tirades. Still, I couldn't see why he would kill a pirate and leave him in the lighthouse.

Unless it was to possibly get more attention for this upcoming movie?

Because some people did believe that bad publicity was good publicity, and something like this would definitely get attention. But why send out an altered script? That had to be connected to this crime, right? It was the only thing that made sense to me.

And then there were those numbers on the paper found in Bucky's pocket. My name had been on the paper. How did that fit with all of this? It just didn't make any sense.

The next person my gaze fell on was Rick. I'd only talked with him a couple times, but he seemed nice, and he seemed knowledgeable about his job. I supposed I didn't really know enough about him to determine if he had the motive, means, or opportunity to kill Bucky.

Sarah was just out of college and worked for little to no pay. I suppose she could be responsible, but I had no idea why she would do anything like this.

I supposed anybody could be responsible, and I could be poring over suspects for days and days.

Not that anyone had asked me to pore over suspects. In fact, it was quite the opposite. People had asked me *not* to pore over the suspects. But my mind just couldn't help it.

"Joey!" Alistair shouted. "It's your line! Aren't you paying attention?" He snapped his fingers. "I need everything you've got right now. We have no time to waste. This is no time to stare off into space!"

"Don't get your knickers in a twist, Alistair," I said.

Someone gasped nearby.

"I'll get my knickers in a twist if I want to," Alistair stepped closer. "Do you understand?"

I was many things . . . but I wasn't afraid of Alistair. "Twisted knickers aren't a good look on you. A nice sequined pantsuit might do you better."

Someone snickered.

Alistair stared at me, derision in his gaze.

Before he could respond, I flashed a smile. "Now, back to filming, right?"

He stepped back. "Yes, Your Majesty."

Your Majesty? That sounded an awful lot like what someone who might have called me a diva would say. Was Alistair the one who'd leaked information for that article?

I snapped back into character and stared off into the distance.

"Betrayal is like a game of roulette in which no one wins," I whispered, my voice hoarse.

I shuddered.

Why did that statement sound so threatening right now?

———

Just before seven, Alistair released us from filming. He would've kept us longer, but the sun had set and he needed daylight in order to film the scenes. I, for one, was happy to call it quits for the day.

As the crew began packing up, I started toward my trailer. Washington and Eva had already left. The last few scenes had been just me, talking to my imaginary friend.

I was exhausted. Partly because I hadn't slept last night. However, being out in the sun and on my feet for hours, and working with Alistair, when put together, left me feeling as bushed as a chicken on a treadmill.

When I'd initially read the script—well, *read* was a strong word. It was more like I'd skimmed it—I thought it seemed decent. But now that we were really diving into it, I wondered what this would do for my career.

It wasn't my normal action-packed adventure. No, the scenes were slow. The dialogue was heavy. The twist . . . well, I still wasn't sure what to think about the twist. People would either love it or hate it.

This film will be the death of you.

Was that literal or figurative?

I knew it was too late to get out of this. I had signed a contract and agreed to do the film. So I needed to carry it out. But I wasn't happy with the way things were progressing.

Jackson rose to join me but paused on the steps to my RV. "I'll wait out here."

"I won't be long," I told him.

I stepped into my trailer and walked over to my

dresser so I could change out of my costume. A strange paper sat on top of the wood there.

I paused, almost not wanting to know what it was. But I couldn't stop myself from picking it up—while only holding the corner with a tissue, of course.

I blinked at what I saw there.

It was a picture of me, dressed as Drusilla. Below the photo were the words, "A picture of a dead woman."

CHAPTER
THIRTEEN

AFTER TRANSFORMING BACK INTO JOEY, I put the threatening picture into my purse and met Jackson outside. He stood with his hands in his pockets, the lighthouse and beach behind him. He was a very nice distraction from all the bad things that had happened.

At the moment, he struck me as someone who could be in the scene of a very romantic movie. He could easily be a swoon-worthy hero waiting to sweep someone off her feet. I loved it even more that he wasn't the Hollywood type. He was so grounded in reality that I halfway expected Julie Chen to show up and give commentary on his life.

Jackson's eyes lit when he saw me. That was something worthy of a movie itself. There was nothing like seeing that look of love in his eyes. It never failed to warm me through and through.

He stepped closer and planted a kiss on my cheek. "Are you ready to go?"

"Wherever you're going sounds like a good place to be," I told him.

He grinned. "That's what I like to hear."

We climbed into his truck. He cranked the engine, but we just sat there for a moment. I could see the last remains of dusk in the distance, and it was beautiful with its muted gray and pink.

I could watch this all day. Especially with Jackson.

I almost didn't want to bring up the picture that had been left on my dresser. I didn't want to ruin the moment. But I knew I couldn't keep this information from him.

I frowned as I pulled the paper from my purse. "This was left in my trailer."

His eyes widened as he looked at it. "You just found this?"

I nodded.

His expression darkened. "Someone was in your trailer. I don't like that."

"Me neither. But it seems to confirm your theory that someone in this cast or crew is involved."

"You didn't see anyone lingering around it, did you?"

"I didn't."

Silence fell for a minute.

"Should I tell the police?" I finally asked.

"Of course. Speaking of which, you might have the perfect opportunity. I know this is kind of last minute, but Chief Chambers—or Cassidy, as she told me to call her—asked if we wanted to do dinner with her and her husband tonight."

"That sounds like fun."

"I think so too. We don't know each other well, but it would be fun to get to know her. You know law enforcement—we're all one big family sometimes."

Staying occupied would keep me out of trouble and stop me from running around town looking for answers and clues that I wasn't supposed to be hunting. That seemed like a good idea to me.

"Okay, great. Do you need to go back to your place and get changed?"

I glanced down at the jeans and T-shirt I wore. Normally I would want to put on some fresh makeup and maybe even fix my hair. But, for some strange reason, I felt okay looking like I did.

Maybe dressing up like Drusilla Fairweather was teaching me a few things about the importance of working on character makeovers rather than physical transformations.

"No, I think I'm fine going like I am."

"I think you're beautiful, however you look."

"Warts and all?"

He grinned. "Warts and all."

"So, Joey," Cassidy said over dinner, "I have to say, I love your TV show, *Relentless*. I'm not much on watching TV, nor do I really have a lot of time. But that is one series that I've binge watched."

Cassidy grabbed a roll from the center of the table as we sat outside on the deck, a nice ocean breeze floating around us. Their dog, Kujo, a golden retriever, sat beside us and made me miss Ripley. Ripley was Jackson's Australian shepherd. A friend from the police station was taking care of him while Jackson was here.

A surge of satisfaction rose in me at Cassidy's words. She said she loved my show.

I was proud of my work on *Relentless*. That was a good thing since I'd dedicated years of my life to it. "Thanks. I love hearing that."

"She's telling the truth," her husband, Ty, said. "I've never seen her so addicted to a TV show."

He cast Cassidy a glance that was clearly full of love and adoration. I could practically see cartoon hearts floating between them. It was sweet.

The two of them lived in a little cottage right on the ocean. The place was nothing fancy. But they'd recently done some upgrades and added some cabanas at the back of their property. A welcoming, homey vibe surrounded us.

I'd learned that Cassidy's husband, Ty, was a former Navy SEAL, and he had started an organization here called Hope House for wounded veterans and military. He sponsored the participants to come here and helped facilitate their inner healing. It was a noble calling.

I loved being here this evening. Moments like these were what I wanted for my life—simple moments sharing a meal, enjoying the weather, and spending time with interesting people. Cassidy and Ty seem like the perfect people to do it with. They were both welcoming and kind, and there was nothing not to like about them.

It was nice also because Jackson and Cassidy could talk their police work stuff. Ty interjected, sharing his experiences as a SEAL. I listened to everything, putting a mental "research" stamp on it all.

But, just as I hoped, as Ty pulled out coffee and blueberry cheesecake, the conversation turned to what was going on here on the island right now—the death of Bucky Belching.

"So, if you don't mind me asking," Jackson started. "Are there any updates on the case?"

I'd never been so proud. I'd *so* been hoping somebody would bring it up.

Cassidy took a sip of her coffee before saying, "I've been looking into it all day and talking to people and trying to piece together what happened in the moments leading up to his death."

"Did you discover his real name yet?" I asked, before taking another bite of my cheesecake. The creamy, sugary goodness practically melted on my tongue.

As Cassidy set her mug on the table and leaned back, Ty draped his arm around the back of her chair, creating an idyllic picture.

A picture that I wanted for my own future.

The two of them just seemed so settled and happy. Would this ever be Jackson and me?

"No, it's strange," Cassidy said. "This guy had no driver's license or credit cards. His fingerprints weren't in the system. Even his car belongs to someone up in New Jersey. The owner apparently is out of the country, and I haven't been able to get in touch with him."

"How about his personal belongings?" Jackson asked. "Any leads there?"

"That's the other strange thing," Cassidy said. "It

almost seems as if someone came, grabbed all his things, and got rid of them. There's a chance they could have been dumped in the ocean and we'll never find them."

"Sounds like you've dealt with stuff like this before." I pulled my sweater around my shoulders as the breeze turned cooler.

"Unfortunately, I have."

"Is there anything you can share about Corky?" I asked. "Were you able to look into him?"

She picked up her phone and showed me a picture of the man. "Here he is. Real name is Terry Keeling. He had an alibi for the evening."

I stared at the picture a moment. I was pretty sure Corky Keelhauler was the man I'd earlier referred to as Blackbeard. He'd been part of the mob that had stormed the set.

Cassidy paused. "Joey, is there anybody on set that you can think of who might want to sabotage things?"

"I've been thinking about that all day, to be truthful," I told them. "I mean, I suppose if you dig deeply enough, anybody could have a motive."

"So you haven't seen anybody fighting or arguing?" Cassidy asked. "Nothing specific?"

I remembered what Mindy told me about Eva and Alistair being an item. Remembered Washington's drinking problem. Were either of those things significant? I had no idea. I wasn't even sure I should bring it up. Both things were hearsay.

"There's really nothing that I know of," I finally told her. "But if I learn anything, you'll be the first one I tell."

Cassidy straightened. "That sounds like a plan."

"Tell her about the picture," Jackson said.

Cassidy cast a curious look at me. "Picture?"

After a moment of hesitation, I pulled it from my purse. I'd left the tissue with it, just in case there were prints. "This was left for me."

"Who is that a picture of?" Ty asked.

"That's me. In character."

He squinted before nodding and letting out an indiscernible grunt.

I really needed to get used to that reaction.

"I'll test this for fingerprints," Cassidy said.

I nodded. But all I could see were the words "dead woman."

CHAPTER
FOURTEEN

JACKSON and I climbed back into his truck after dinner. It was ten o'clock, and I was beat. But I was really glad that we had gone over to the Chambers's place. It had been good to talk to Cassidy and Ty, and, for a moment, it had felt like Jackson and I were a normal couple with a normal life on a normal outing.

As I pulled on my seatbelt, I wondered what it would be like just to have a regular life with Jackson. To have a regular schedule where we were together day in and day out. To be able to see my fiancé every day.

Instead, I was out of town for weeks at a time. Even when I was in town, Jackson worked his crazy shifts. It depended on his caseload, but policing wasn't a 9-to-5 job type of thing.

Jackson pulled away from their house and started down the dark road.

Would I ever be happy just settling down and having a normal life? Maybe. I wasn't sure. I wanted to say yes. But there was another part of me that knew I loved acting and Hollywood and that it was where I was meant to be.

The question was, could I have it both ways? Could I have a normal life with Jackson and live as a Hollywood actress? That was the dilemma I'd been struggling with ever since we'd been engaged.

"I guess you want to get back to your house?" Jackson's voice cut through the silence.

My thoughts raced. I knew I should say yes. I knew he *expected* me to say yes. But there was one other place I wanted to go.

"Actually, can we make one stop?"

He looked at me, a wrinkle forming between his eyes. "Is this about the murder?"

I couldn't lie to him—even if I wanted to. "Well, maybe. It's hard to say. It's just this feeling I have in my gut. I want to see if anything pans out."

"You want to investigate, in other words." He raised his eyebrows, a knowing look in his eyes.

"Yes, I suppose I do. But when I say *investigate*, I don't mean to *actually* investigate. I mean, I just want to *gather information*."

Didn't that sound much better than saying it the other way? That was what I told myself. I mean, I wouldn't be confronting anybody or anything. I just wanted to collect facts. That wasn't a bad thing, right?

"You told Cassidy that you didn't know anything," Jackson reminded me. "Is there something you're not saying?"

"I *don't* know anything. But Mindy, who is my makeup artist, told me that Alistair might be seeing someone in the cast."

Jackson shot me a quick glance before looking back at the road. "You didn't think *that* was relevant enough to tell Cassidy?"

"I wasn't sure, but I don't want to start rumors. I mean, there are lots and lots of rumors out there. Believe me—I'm usually in the middle of those rumors, me and my 'diva self.'" I still felt bitter about that article about me. "I just thought maybe we could swing by Alistair's place and see if he's there alone. I don't want to go inside. I don't want to talk to anyone. I just want to watch. Could you just give me like an hour to do that?"

"It's an hour that you want to spend watching from my truck, correct? And only from my truck?"

"Yes, that's correct. That's all I want to do. Watch and observe. Stay in the shadows. Out of trouble."

He let out a breath and ran a hand over his face.

I thought for sure he was going to say no and head back to my place.

Instead, he said in a teasingly reluctant voice, "That would mean I get to spend an hour in the truck alone with you?"

That was one way to look at it. My heart lifted. "Yes, exactly. We get to spend *alone* time together . . . while doing surveillance."

Was there anything more romantic?

Jackson glanced at me again. "And you're probably not going to be able to stop thinking about this until you actually do it, correct?"

He could read me like a book. "Unfortunately, yes."

He lightly hit the brakes and peered at the road ahead. "Okay, then. Where is this Alistair guy staying?"

"I just happened to overhear his address earlier."

"Just happened?" He raised his eyebrows.

"Of course. I would never eavesdrop or anything."

He chuckled. "No, never."

We pulled up to Alistair's oceanfront mega mansion. He'd told me I was the only one staying in a big house fit for a star. He apparently considered himself a star also, because his house may have even been bigger than mine.

Though it was dark, I could make out some details. The place appeared to be a lovely two-story structure located at the edge of the water, with massive dunes behind it.

Jackson, being the consummate professional that he was, had turned his lights off as we approached the house. He pulled over on the side of the road, cut the engine, and now we stared at the place.

The lights were on up on the second floor, and the curtains appeared to be open. I hoped that meant we'd be able to see something inside. But the fact remained that there was only one car outside the house.

Jackson and I sat back, ready to settle in for the next hour of watching. He had already been through the drill with me. I knew that doing a stakeout wasn't nearly as exciting as it seemed on TV.

They were tedious. They were boring. They required holding your bladder for hours on end— much like wearing a body suit. There was nothing glamourous about it.

But if there was anybody that I wanted to do this with, it was Jackson.

"So . . ." Jackson leaned back, a swath of moonlight illuminating his profile. "Is it always like that on set?"

"What do you mean?"

"That Alistair guy seems like a real jerk. It took every part of my self-control not to jump out of my seat and give him a piece of my mind when he started talking down to you."

Hooray for chivalry. I, for one, loved it.

"Well, Alistair can be a jerk. Not everybody is like that. One of my friends—Starla McKnight—was on the set once, and she just cried and cried and cried because the director kept talking down to her. It was awful. She couldn't wait for that movie to be done."

"Why didn't she just drop out?"

"It's not quite as easy as it might seem. Sure, sometimes you hear rumors about how awful some people are to work with. But then the opportunity comes along or the right script and . . . I don't know." I shrugged. "Maybe common sense goes out the window. I don't really know. Maybe you just want to believe the best in people, and you believe the people who were telling the stories are just exaggerating. I don't know why we do the things we do sometimes."

"As happy as I am to see you, I can't wait for you

to be finished filming. I know it's only the second day, but I'm already not loving this."

"The truth is, I'm not loving this movie," I admitted. "But the contract is signed."

"I know you said that movies like this one could help your career," Jackson said. "But the script is just so strange. Then again, I don't know the business like you do."

"Believe me, I'm questioning this decision. I should've said no, and I should've taken these two weeks to go to Nags Head and spend time with you." I grabbed his hand and squeezed it. The spicy scent of his cologne made me want to lean closer and stay there.

"It's okay, Joey."

I barely heard him. "I'm sorry I didn't. I guess the opportunity was dangling in front of me, and it seemed too good to pass up. But, the truth is, you're too good to pass up. I appreciate the fact that you were willing to compromise and come out here instead."

He swiped a hair behind my ear and gazed at me. "You know I'm your biggest fan. I want to support you however I can."

"How is it really going, Jackson?" My voice turned serious. "How are you doing with the long-distance thing? I know we've talked about it. I know we chat on the phone all the time. But I really want to know how you're feeling. This lifestyle . . . it's not easy."

His lips pressed together. "I'm not going to lie. It's hard. It's hard when my friends have people to go home to or out to dinner with, and I'm there by myself. But I'm a big boy. I can handle this. You're worth the wait."

But what if this period in our lives wasn't just a period? What would happen if this schedule was long-term? I kept those questions to myself.

Maybe I didn't ask because I didn't want to know. I wasn't sure. I only knew I didn't have it all figured out yet.

As the thoughts weighed heavily on my mind, I continued to watch Alistair's house. I straightened when I saw movement there. It was Alistair.

I grabbed Jackson's binoculars for a better look. I spotted him through the upstairs window. I was guessing he might be in the kitchen, based on what looked like cabinets in the background. And, again, this was all conjecture, but it almost looked like he was at the sink, maybe washing dishes.

That was when I saw somebody else come up behind him and wrap her long arms around his waist. He turned around, and the two kissed.

I squinted, trying to see the woman's features. But

I couldn't even get a good glimpse at the woman's hair color. Was that Eva? She was the only person who made sense. Maybe Mindy had been correct.

Was this the information that I had been looking for? Did it mean anything? I didn't know.

But someone had motive, means, and opportunity for murder. I just needed to figure out who.

CHAPTER
FIFTEEN

"WHAT IF ALISTAIR brought somebody with him? Did you ever think about that?" Jackson leaned back in the truck, seeming unbothered by our extended stay in his vehicle as we staked out Alistair's place. This was all in a day's work for him.

"I mean, I suppose that is a possibility." I tried to lean back and look equally as comfortable. Unfortunately, I already had the urge to stretch my legs, grab an overpriced cup of coffee, and maybe look into renting a Porta Potty. "Or it could be somebody suspicious."

Jackson rubbed his chin and shook his head. "Just because Alistair might be seeing someone doesn't really implicate him in a murder."

"I realize that," I said. "But it might speak to his character."

Jackson glanced at me, his eyebrows raised. "I think you already know what his character is. You've made it clear you don't think highly of him."

I frowned, realizing he had a great point. "That's true. Like I said, I'm just in the investigating and gathering information stage. I'm a hunter and a gatherer." I said the words dramatically, like I was narrating a documentary on Native Americans or something.

Jackson gave me one of his no-nonsense looks that I'd become accustomed to. "People did those things in the past as a matter of survival."

"I am trying to survive." I shrugged, realizing the stark truth of my words.

Jackson frowned at me, that familiar worry filling his gaze. My words had struck a nerve, hadn't they? I was in danger . . . again.

"Unless you want to stick around here tonight to figure out exactly who this is, I say you let me take you back to your place." Jackson straightened and reached for his key in the ignition.

I glanced at the window again. Alistair and the mystery woman had disappeared from sight. Her face had been obscured, and I couldn't confirm who it was. The more I thought about it, the more certain I was that it had to be Eva.

The measures people would go to in order to get what they wanted never ceased to astound me.

But Jackson was right. This didn't really prove anything about our investigation. Despite that, Alistair remained in my mind as a suspect.

Jackson pulled away, headed back to my place.

As he did, headlights appeared behind us.

Headlights?

I straightened, keeping watch to see if this was a coincidence or more.

As the vehicle came right up on our tail, I knew it wasn't.

I glanced over at Jackson and saw his jaw tighten. He and I were on the same wavelength.

That vehicle was bad news.

I gripped the armrest and glanced back. The headlights were so bright I couldn't make out anything about the vehicle. I'd thought it was a car earlier, but now I was thinking it was a truck, based on the height alone.

"Hold on, Joey," Jackson muttered, his hands gripping the steering wheel.

I was going to hold on all right. I might even close my eyes and mutter some prayers.

He charged down the road.

"Shouldn't you turn off onto a side street to lose them?" I asked.

"Most of these side streets are dead ends," he said.

"So what are we going to do? Have a drag race down the highway?" That sounded like a terrible idea.

"No, but I have another idea."

Jackson jerked his truck to the left, onto one of those very side streets.

When I saw a house at the end, I repressed a shudder.

What was he thinking?

I glanced behind us again.

The other vehicle was still there.

It was a good thing I trusted Jackson. A really good thing.

Because, right now, it looked like he was charging toward the house and going to crash into it.

I decided maybe I should close my eyes.

Suddenly, we jerked again. I felt a bump. A shift. And then we charged forward again.

When I opened my eyes, we were on the beach, driving on the sand. "What . . . ?"

"You can drive off-road here," Jackson said. "But, unless you're experienced, you'll get stuck."

I veered my head around, glancing behind me again.

The vehicle chasing us had stopped.

I let out a breath.

It appeared that we'd lost them.

For now.

But why had someone come after us? What sense did that even make?

I had no idea. but this whole thing was becoming more twisted all the time.

CHAPTER
SIXTEEN

THE NEXT MORNING, I woke up at the crack of dawn feeling totally and completely exhausted. Thankfully, Washington George was going to film some scenes that didn't require me this morning, so I didn't have to be on set until nine. I snuggled back under the covers. The extra sleep would help me think more clearly.

As I pulled my eyes open and slapped my alarm until it quieted, I glanced around.

A stuffed animal stared at me—a llama wearing a T-shirt that read "No Drama." My friend Phoebe had given it to me.

I smiled.

It fit my friend, and I think it was her quiet way of telling me to stay out of trouble.

With a yawn, I stood. Instantly, my thoughts went to the script. Was there a new one this morning?

I scrambled across the room and opened my computer. Quickly, I went to my emails and scanned them.

Voilà! There it was. A revised script.

I clicked on the link and scanned the new document, looking for any changes.

I gasped when I realized what had been altered.

In yesterday's version, Tabitha—played by Eva—had disappeared. In this version of the script, she turned up dead at the end. I felt the color leave my face.

Was I reading into things too much? This didn't necessarily mean that somebody else in real life would die, right?

I wanted to assure myself of that, but I couldn't. Because I knew what reality most likely was.

Somebody else was going to die.

Maybe it wouldn't be today.

Maybe it wouldn't even be tomorrow.

But somebody was planning another murder.

A sick feeling gurgled in my gut.

I resisted the impulse to quickly throw my clothes on, rush downstairs, and wake up Jackson to tell him the news. He had stayed here last night to keep an eye on things. Besides, I had plenty of room here.

Instead of being irrational and having a knee-jerk reaction, I showered and got dressed. Afterward, I calmly padded down the hall to the kitchen. As I glanced outside, I saw the gloomy day there. It seemed fitting for the altered script I'd just gotten.

When I went to the counter, I saw that the coffee had already been started. My spirits lifted. Somebody knew how to speak my love language.

No sooner had I taken a mug from the cabinet and started pouring my cup did I hear somebody behind me. I didn't even have to turn around. Instead, I felt arms wrap around my waist and lips nuzzle my neck.

"Good morning," Jackson murmured. "I thought I heard you get up. By the way, you smell really good."

My heart warmed at his words. I loved his closeness and his warmth and the words that he murmured in my ears.

I turned around to face him, barely an inch between us. I stared into his eyes before planting a kiss on his lips. "How'd you sleep?"

He shrugged. "You know, about as well as I usually do when I keep an ear open for trouble."

I grabbed my cup of coffee and handed it to him. "You should get the first cup."

"Thank you." He took a sip and backed away.

I grabbed a new mug and poured myself some hot coffee. Then we walked over to the patio doors that overlooked the ocean. "It looks nasty out there today, doesn't it?"

"It sure does," Jackson said.

"By the way, I got a new script this morning." I said the words casually, in a no drama llama type of way.

His eyes lit. "Did you?"

"I did. And get this. In this version, someone mysteriously disappears, only to turn up dead at the end."

His eyebrows shot up even higher. "Is that right? You need to tell Cassidy."

"I know. I will. I thought I would wait until it was a little later. I mean, it's not an emergency. Maybe."

"Hopefully, this is just an empty threat, and somebody is playing with us. But, given the fact one person has already died, I wouldn't put it past anyone."

"I know. My thoughts are the same."

Just as I said that, my phone buzzed. I looked

down and saw I had a text message from Alistair. My gaze scanned the words there.

"Filming has been delayed again today," I told Jackson. "Alistair said there's nothing we can do in these kinds of weather conditions, but that we should study our script. He made it a point to say the *original* script, almost like he knows there could've been another new one."

"Do you think Alistair has anything to do with this?"

I leaned against the counter and let out a breath. "I can't see where that would benefit him in any way. I mean, this is his script. He wrote it, and he's producing it, and he's directing it. The new script is just messing with people's minds. Why would he want to do that when he's in such a rush to get this done?"

"I agree. This whole thing has me baffled."

As soon as the words left Jackson's mouth, my doorbell rang. Jackson and I exchanged a look.

"Who could be here at this time?" I glanced at the clock. It was only eight a.m.

"Stay here," Jackson told me.

I didn't argue. I remained in the kitchen but peered out to see whatever was happening.

With his shoulders tight and stiff, Jackson walked to the front door. As he moved, I saw a gun tucked into his waistband. I shouldn't be surprised. He hardly went anywhere without one, and now he was going to be especially prone to having it close because of everything that happened.

I held my breath as he opened the door. And I could not believe who I saw on the other side.

CHAPTER
SEVENTEEN

I SUCKED in a breath before exclaiming, "Dizzy! Geraldine! MaryAnn! Maxine! What in the world are you guys doing here?"

Dizzy extended her arms and pulled me into a long, motherly hug. "We heard you were close so we just had to come see you. How are you? You're getting so skinny. Aren't they feeding you on set?"

Her friends yattered in agreement.

"So thin."

"What's your secret?"

"Did it involve swallowing cotton balls?"

Right now, I could hardly breathe. Dizzy squeezed me so hard my innards begged for mercy. Finally, she released me, and I was able to croak out, "I am fine. Same weight. No secrets. Definitely no cotton balls."

I glanced at my friends. Man, did I love them. Especially Dizzy.

She was actually my aunt by marriage, and she'd been there for me through some tough times. She had a trademark bright-blue eyeshadow she liked to wear all the way up to her eyebrows. Her hair was styled big and into something that reminded me of a beehive.

She was a hoot, and I couldn't believe she was actually here.

Jackson gave everyone hugs as well, and then we all stepped back.

"How did you even find me?" I asked Dizzy, holding onto her arm.

"Oh, it was easy." Dizzy fluttered her hand in the air. "As soon as we got off the ferry, we stopped at the first gas station, and we asked the people who work there. Apparently, everyone here on the island knows exactly where you're staying. What can I say? It's a small town, and that's the price you pay for being so popular and cute."

I exchanged another look with Jackson. That was not comforting. There were definitely times when privacy was a great thing to be had. Especially, let's say, when a killer might be looking for you.

I'd had it happen to me enough in the past that I was now sufficiently cautious.

I went through and greeted the rest of the gang. There was Maxine, who owned a great secondhand store called Utter Clutter; Geraldine, who'd been a homemaker; and MaryAnn, a retired teacher. All were in their late fifties or early sixties, and together they called themselves the Hot Chicks.

My gaze shifted when I saw movement behind them. Two others trudged up the stairs, towing suitcases behind them. My heart pounded with excitement.

"Phoebe?" I mumbled as she pulled me into a hug.

"It's so good to see you, Joey. I've missed you."

"Zane?"

Zane Oakley wrapped his arms around me. "The ladies convinced me to be their chauffeur. I just happened to be getting a haircut from Dizzy yesterday when she mentioned this trip. I was like, hashtag: definitely."

"I'm glad you did. This is quite a surprise. You guys must've caught an early ferry."

"We heard that the weather might get bad later in the day," Dizzy said. "So we knew if we were going to come it had to be sooner rather than later."

"Smart thinking."

I stepped back and looked at Jackson as he coolly surveyed Zane. The two men had an interesting history. They'd both wanted to date me, but, obviously, Jackson had won. Things had been tense between them since then.

The two were polar opposites. Zane had curly hair that bounced away from his face in a white guy afro. He had the thin, lean build of a surfer, though he worked as both a real estate agent and massage therapist to pay the bills. We shared a love of smoothies and Bob Ross.

Zane and I were just friends—good friends. Not as good of friends as we *had* been. That would be weird now that I was engaged. But Zane would always be special to me.

"Well," I said, turning back to my unexpected guests. "Everybody, it's great to have you here. What do you say we make some breakfast? After all, my plans were just canceled for today, so let's have a good time and catch up."

The next three hours were spent making breakfast and talking to everyone. I couldn't even begin to tell how much good it did my heart to see everybody from home. I hadn't even realized I was homesick, but I clearly was.

As unfortunate as it was that filming had been

pushed back, the distraction had been good. I didn't know what it would mean for my schedule going forward. The movie needed to be completed, and I needed to be back on the set of *Relentless* in less than two weeks. I could see where it might be problematic, but, for the moment, I was not going to worry about it.

As we were all sitting on the deck talking, my doorbell rang. Who now? Almost everybody I knew was here at my place already.

Jackson walked with me to answer it. I secretly loved this protective side of him.

I had no idea what to expect when I opened the door. But it hadn't been seeing Eva standing there in her rainboots, holding a teardrop umbrella, with a deep frown etched onto her face.

"Hello," I said, uncertainty in my voice. "This is quite a . . . surprise."

As much as I didn't like the woman, I couldn't help but notice a concerned look on her face. I had a feeling something was going on. It was the only reason she would have shown up here.

"Hi, Joey. Jackson." She nodded at both of us. "I know this is weird. I'm sorry to come over like this. But I needed someone to talk to. Do you guys have a minute?"

I hated to question her intentions. I really did. But

I didn't know if I could trust this woman or if she had ulterior motives.

Despite my hesitations and concerns, I opened the door wider and let her come inside. While the rest of my friends were on the deck enjoying each other's company, I sat down with Eva and Jackson in the dining room so I could listen to her concerns.

She shifted in the chair before her gaze fluttered up to meet mine and then Jackson's. "I keep feeling like somebody's watching me."

"What do you mean?" I questioned.

"I mean, you got the new script, right?"

"I did," I told her.

"Then I'm sure you read the new scene that had been added."

"I did. Your character disappears and turns up dead in this new version."

As soon as I said the words, she seemed to instantly tighten. "I know this is going to sound weird. I just know it is, but, the truth is, I think I might actually disappear."

CHAPTER
EIGHTEEN

I GLANCED at Jackson as Eva's somber words filled the dining room.

"Why in the world would you think that, Eva?" I leaned closer, suddenly not feeling as laid-back. Even my friends' laughter in the background did little to help my muscles relax.

"I know it sounds crazy." Eva waved her hands near her eyes, as if fighting tears. "I do. But ever since I got here, I have felt like somebody has been watching me. And then I got some dead roses delivered to my door."

"Dead roses?" Jackson echoed.

She nodded. "Yes, and there was a note for me with them."

Jackson shifted in his chair and leaned on the

table, his full attention on Eva. "What did the note say, Eva?"

"It said, I have my eye on you." She shivered and glanced out the window. "I don't even know what that means. There's no way someone said that trying to sound sweet, right? It's just creepy. And then there are the dead roses. There's no mistaking their meaning."

I rubbed my arms, suddenly feeling chilled myself. "When did you find the roses?"

"This morning when I opened the door."

Did that mean she'd been home all evening? Or had she actually found them when she got home from Alistair's? "Do you have any idea who might have sent them?"

"No, I have no idea." She frowned and stared across the table at Jackson and me. "All of this has me shaking. I know that you're used to things like this, Joey. But this is new territory for me."

Jackson leaned back, and I could see him processing all of this. "Did you tell the police?"

"Not yet. I feel like they already have so much going on."

"You should file a report, just in case," Jackson said.

Eva nodded, still looking a little dazed. "I will."

Jackson lifted a pencil from a basket on the table

and tapped it in his hands. "Is this your first time working with most of this cast and crew, Eva?"

"As a matter of fact, it's not. I had a role in Alistair's last movie, and he kept a lot of the same crew he had last time."

I remembered what Mindy had told me about Eva being with Alistair so she could get these roles. Was what Mindy said true? I kept that information in the back of my mind.

"Throughout all of that, you didn't have any hostility with any of the other cast or crew members?" Jackson continued.

Eva fluttered her eyelashes and shrugged. "Not really. But, to be truthful, I don't think Washington George likes me."

"Washington George?" His was the last name I expected to hear. "Why do you say that?"

"I don't know. There's just something about him. I caught him staring at me, muttering something under his breath. It was just kind of weird." Her face scrunched into a pouty look that had been perfected by the actors of *Mean Girls*.

"Do you think he might have been staring at you because he's attracted to you?" Jackson asked.

"Look, I've had plenty of guys check me out. It was different than that. There was just something about the look in his eyes that's got me a little shaken."

"So you think he's a viable suspect in this?" I just didn't see it. Then again, I didn't know Washington that well. Maybe I should be more open-minded.

"I don't know," Eva lowered her gaze, and put a fisted hand over her mouth, the picture of anguish.

Was she acting? I knew all about that.

But I couldn't gauge her sincerity level right now.

"I don't want to point fingers at anyone," Eva continued. "But I also don't want to get dead roses or notes saying that someone is keeping their eye on me. It's just creepy. This whole thing is creepy. Somebody is going to a lot of trouble to send us these revised scripts. It doesn't make any sense to me."

At least that was one thing two of us could agree on. It *was* creepy.

"Do you think Washington George could be responsible for altering the script?" I asked.

"I hate to say it, but I don't think he has the smarts to do it."

"So you think there are two different people at work here?" Jackson asked. "One who's rewriting the script and another who's threatening the cast?"

Eva shrugged. "To be honest, I have no idea."

I leaned forward. There was a question I had to ask her. I wasn't going to hold back, especially since she'd come to me for help. "Eva, are you and Alistair secretly seeing each other?"

Her eyes widened. "Why would you ask that?"

"I'm just wondering. If you want our help, I need you to be forthcoming."

"That's none of your business." Her voice turned from helpless to hardened.

"Okay, then, I'm not really sure that we can do anything to help you." I stood as if ready to walk away. I knew how to play hard ball when needed.

"No," Eva called. "Please. Don't. I really do need your help."

I paused and turned toward her. "Then I need you to be truthful with me. Are you and Alistair seeing each other? Were you at his house last night?"

Her eyes widened even more. "Last night? No, I was not there last night. Last night, I needed all the sleep I could get. I went to bed at nine. I can't have myself looking awful on the set. There's only room for one person to look awful on the set." She smirked.

I felt my face scrunching together in a scowl. "You really don't think you can say stuff like that and expect me to be nice to you, right?"

My father had highlighted verses in his Bible about loving your enemies. About turning the other cheek. But that had to be one of the hardest things in the whole world to do.

There was a fine line between standing up for yourself and not being walked on, and turning the other cheek. I'd yet to perfect it. I wasn't sure if I ever would.

Eva released a long sigh and did a half eye roll. "Okay, look, I'm sorry. I just think it's hysterical that you have to wear that getup every day. Everyone knows you're gorgeous. But now you get a taste of what regular people feel."

"Oh, come on. Can you really say that?" I stared at Eva, wondering what kind of game she was playing. "I mean, you're gorgeous too. You have no room to talk."

Her gaze narrowed. "Since we're being honest here and you want me to be truthful, let me just tell you this. At twelve, I went on my first diet. At sixteen, I had a nose job. At twenty-one, I had liposuction. I've had numerous other procedures to get to this look. I work out for two hours daily, and only eat around eight hundred calories a day."

All I could do was grunt in surprise. Her truthful moment had gained her points with me. It couldn't be easy to say that, especially in front of a guy she appeared to be crushing on.

I cleared my throat. "So you're telling me that you were not with Alistair last night?"

Eva nodded. "That's correct. I was not with Alistair. We dated each other for a few weeks, if you want to call it that. Really, it was more like a fling. I really thought we had something, but, apparently, Alistair didn't see it that way. He's not the type who wants to be tied down to one person. If you think he was with someone last night, it wasn't me. I have no way of proving it. I'm staying by myself. All you have is my word."

Despite my dislike for Eva, I had to admit that I believed her.

Whatever was going on inside this movie was just strange. And we needed to get to the bottom of it before more people got hurt.

In the early afternoon, the crowd at my place all decided to go out to eat. I was never much of a cook, and I didn't have that many groceries. So I decided to introduce the whole gang to the delight known as The Crazy Chefette.

Even Eva decided to come along with us. She and Zane seemed to connect, which didn't surprise me. The two of them were going to ride together in Jackson's truck to the restaurant, Jackson was going to drive the Hot Chicks, and Phoebe and I were going to take my Miata so we could catch up alone for a few minutes.

Phoebe was actually Jackson's sister-in-law. Or his former sister-in-law. I wasn't sure how all that worked in reality. But Phoebe's sister, Claire, had been Jackson's first wife, who had died from cancer. The two were still close.

Phoebe was basically my opposite. Where I was emotional and dramatic and liked to be the center of attention and to insert my nose where it didn't belong, Phoebe was quiet and chill and perfectly content to remain in the background. She loved animals, which was why she had her own pet-sitting business. But she also worked at a smoothie shack in the summertime.

She'd recently begun dating my friend Sam Butler. Sam was my costar on *Relentless,* and the two had hit it off when he had come to visit me in Nags Head this past summer.

As we drove to The Crazy Chefette, I needed an update from her.

"So, what's going on with you and Sam?"

Her face seemed to light up with happiness as soon as I said his name.

"Sam is great," she told me. "As you know, we

don't get to see each other that much, but we call each other every day. I think I'm going to go to see him next week. He had to fly back to California for something this week, then he's going to come out to Nags Head."

"That's great, Phoebe. I know he's going to be happy to see you. He talks about you all the time between takes on the set. He really seems smitten."

"Smitten? I like that word." Phoebe flashed a smile.

I grinned. I'd missed my friend, and I was happy for her. "It's so wonderful to see you again. You look like you're really doing great."

"Oh, I am. No complaints. Well, except maybe that I don't get to see you often enough. We are really missing you back at home."

At her words, my heart squeezed. "I miss you all too. I really do. I'm going to get my schedule figured out here soon. I know that I am."

My problem was that I was an all-or-nothing type of girl. And, right now, I was in my all phase. That "all" involved acting instead of my relationships.

"I know Jackson misses you," Phoebe said. She opened her mouth, as if about to say something else, but she stopped herself.

"What is it?" I gripped the steering wheel as I followed behind Jackson, my curiosity growing.

"Nothing."

"That nothing clearly means there's something."

She hesitated. "I was just going to tell you that I stopped by Jackson's the other day. He was watching *Relentless*."

I smiled at the thought. "Was he?"

Phoebe nodded. "He sure was . . . it was weird, though. He looked . . . sad."

My smile disappeared. "Sad? What do you mean?"

"I think he's struggling with you being gone, Joey, probably more than he'll ever admit."

"I miss him too."

"I know you do. It's just that . . . why be with someone if you can't actually be with them, right? Isn't that the point of finding someone you want to do life together with?"

My heart pounded in my ears as her words settled over me. "Yes, I guess it is. But people make long-distance relationships work all the time. Absence makes the heart grow fonder, right?"

She waved a hand in the air. "Yes, of course. I'm sorry. I don't know why I brought it up. Maybe it isn't as much you and Jackson I'm thinking about. Maybe I'm taking all these feelings and emotions I have toward Sam and I'm deflecting them on you and Jackson."

I didn't know if that was true or not, but her words caused a subtle ache in my heart. I'd think about it later. At the moment, I wanted to concentrate on my friend. "It sounds like you and Sam miss each other too."

She frowned. "We do. This long-distance thing is harder than I thought it would be."

"It is hard. I'm sorry." Even as I said the words, my mind went back to what she'd told me.

Jackson looked sad? That was the last thing I wanted for my fiancé. I cared about him too much for him to be sad.

But what was I going to do about it?

I had no idea right now.

We all pulled into the parking lot of the restaurant. We were getting there a bit after the lunch crowd. The owner, a woman named Lisa Dillinger, let us put the tables together so we could sit as a group.

As we did, Mayor Mac MacArthur called out hello to me, Lisa pulled out some food experiments for all of us to sample, and another man—Doc Clemson, I heard someone call him—began serenading anyone listening with a rendition of "Dem Bones."

I almost felt like I was a local, and it was only my second or third day here.

We were talking happily amongst ourselves when I saw a familiar figure walk inside.

Rick.

His eyes searched the room as if looking for some-body before stopping on me.

Great. What now?

He walked over to me, and I could tell something was on his mind.

"Joey," he started. "I need to talk to you. Eva too. Please. If you don't mind."

Eva seemed to be listening because she joined us. We walked with Rick toward the corner of the restaurant where there were no other patrons so we could have some privacy.

"Hey, listen," he started. "I was hoping to find you here."

"How did you know we were here?" I found it a little suspicious myself. Then again, at this moment, I was suspicious of everyone in the cast and crew of the film. Until I had answers, I would remain that way.

"I just happened to be driving past earlier when I saw you guys walk inside. When I came back by this way, I saw the cars were still here so I took a chance."

I suppose that explanation made sense. "Okay, so what's going on?"

"I know this is going to sound weird, but have either of you talked to Alistair today?"

Eva and I glanced at each other, and we both shook our heads.

"No, I just got a text from him this morning about production being postponed," I said.

"Yeah, we all got the text." Rick rubbed the cross-shaped scar on his cheek, his face and eyes tense. "But nobody has seen or talked to him today."

A chill went up my spine at his words. "Wait, so you think something's wrong?"

"I went to his house because I had a question about production. I knocked on the door but nobody answered."

"Did you try his phone?" Eva asked.

"I did. Nobody answered. I even wondered if he could be walking on the beach to blow off some steam. I know it's raining, but people have done stranger things. However, I didn't see him. This isn't like him. When Alistair is filming, his whole world is consumed with his work."

"It sounds like you're worried," I said.

Rick frowned. "I've worked with Alistair for years and probably know him better than anyone on the set. This isn't like him. We work well together because he's demanding, and I'm a perfectionist—or OCD, as he calls me. It's why we make a good team."

Rick did seem like a perfectionist, now that he

mentioned it. And perfectionists generally had an eye for detail . . . details like sudden changes in behavior.

Alistair disappearing definitely seemed strange.

I looked over at Jackson. It didn't look like I would be enjoying my meal for much longer.

CHAPTER
NINETEEN

JACKSON and I decided to do the responsible thing. We called Chief Chambers and told her what was going on. Then he and I took our sandwiches to go, left my car for Phoebe to drive back, and we met Cassidy at Alistair's place.

I promised my friends we would be back soon, and they'd all seemed understanding. They knew me well enough to know this was par for the course.

Cassidy was already at the house when we arrived. Jackson and I met her on the front stoop.

"Anything?" Jackson asked.

"There's no answer." Cassidy's hands went to her hips as she glanced at the deck. "I was just about to walk around the house and see if I could see anything through the windows. Why don't we split up? You two take the second floor, and I'll take the first."

A thrill ran through me. I loved when I was asked to help.

Alistair's house had decks that stretched around all the levels. It should be fairly easy to get an inside view of most of the place, provided that the curtains and blinds were open.

Jackson took my hand and led me up the stairs to the second floor. "I know I've asked this before," he started. "But why does stuff like this always happen to you?"

"I consider everything that happens to me fodder for my acting career."

"That's one way to look at it as the glass being half full."

We reached the second floor. Jackson led me to the first window and cupped his hands around his eyes, peering inside. He did the same for the next several windows, but apparently there was nothing inside to see.

We walked around the corner to the other side of the house. I peered into the patio doors there and sucked in a breath at what I saw.

Alistair lay on the floor.

His legs and hands were bound, and a gag covered his mouth.

His eyes widened when he saw us. He didn't have to say a word for me to hear him loud and clear. He needed our help.

What in the world was going on here?

—————

Ten minutes later, Cassidy had broken inside, we had untied Alistair, and he was now sitting at the kitchen table drinking some coffee. His hands shook, and I could tell he was off-kilter after everything that had happened.

"Why don't you just start at the beginning?" Cassidy held a pad of paper in hand, poised to take notes. "What exactly happened?"

"Do we really have to go through this? Can't you just get out there and find whoever did this?" Alistair's hands shook so hard that coffee sloshed from his mug.

I grabbed a napkin and wiped it up for him.

"I wish it was that easy," Cassidy said. "But I need information first."

"I don't know what to say. All I know is that I was sleeping in my bed. All of a sudden, I felt a shock go through me. It must've been a taser. It's the only thing I can figure."

"Did you see the person who did it?" Chief Chambers asked.

Rain drizzled down the windows behind us, adding to the overall gloomy and gray mood.

"He was wearing a mask, and it was dark," Alistair said. "He didn't say a thing. That almost made it even more disturbing. I have no idea what he wanted."

Chief Chambers shifted in the kitchen chair and continued to study Alistair. "Can you describe him?"

"I don't know." Alistair drew in a shaky breath. "It was too dark to make out any details. He wasn't particularly a big guy. He just seemed average. I know that's not helpful."

"You're doing fine," Cassidy said. "So what happened next?"

"The next thing I knew, this guy was pulling out some duct tape. He put it around my ankles and hands and tied me up. Then he got a towel from the kitchen and shoved it into my mouth." Alistair's voice cracked.

I wasn't used to seeing him like this, and I actually felt bad for him.

"And then?" Chief Chambers asked.

"And then, nothing. No, I take that back. Not nothing." Alistair's eyes lit, and he shook his head. "He grabbed my phone and took it. I have no idea why. I have nothing valuable on it. But he didn't seem to care."

The man had taken Alistair's phone so he could send out that text to the cast and crew. I kept the thought to myself . . . for now. I didn't want to interrupt the flow of Cassidy's questions.

"I'll need you to check the rest of the house to see if anything else was taken that you haven't noticed yet," Chief Chambers said. "Like maybe a computer?"

His eyes darkened. "Do you think that's what this is about? That maybe that man broke in so he could take my computer? Maybe that would somehow make it easier for him to change the script."

Chief Chambers eyeballed him. "You think this is all about the script?"

"It's the only thing that makes sense. Someone is trying to ruin my movie." His hand hit the table, making his coffee quake again.

"Why would someone want to ruin your movie?" Chambers asked. "Does someone have that big of a grudge against you?"

Alistair leaned back, as if trying to remain in control. "I don't know. I've made a lot of enemies throughout the years. I suppose somebody could be doing this as a personal vendetta against me."

"But you have no idea who?" Chief Chambers asked.

"That's right. I have no idea what is going on."

The chief's gaze drifted down the hallway, and her eyes narrowed in thought. "How did you get into the living room?"

"I crawled like an inch worm into the living room. I tried to stand up and open the door so I could somehow get help. But I couldn't. I couldn't do anything. I was forced to lie here and hope that somebody might eventually find me. Then again, maybe my cast and crew are having a little party without me there to oversee them." His nostrils flared as he had a little hissy fit.

I wanted to dislike Alistair even more for his reaction, but I couldn't. I just felt sorry for him.

I cleared my throat, feeling like this was as good a time as any to share an update with Alistair. "Just to let you know, somebody sent a text from your phone saying that filming was delayed today because of the rain."

Alistair's gaze darkened again. "I should've known. See, I tell you someone is trying to ruin my film!"

"I understand that's your theory," Chief Chambers said. "But I'm going to need more than that to go on. I'm going to need you to make a list of anybody you can think of who might have a motive for doing that."

"No problem. I will get right on that. And, in the meantime, I need to get a new phone so I can text my cast and crew and let them know that we need to not waste any more time." His nostrils flared again.

"You're going to have to wait on that." Chief Chambers rose to her feet. "First, I'm going to have to get my guys out here to fingerprint this place and to make sure nothing was left behind. I also need you to make sure that nothing was taken from your place. So slow your roll just a little bit."

Alistair scowled again and crossed his arms. "Fine. But, just for the record, I am not happy about it."

Chief Chambers leaned closer and lowered her voice. "And just for the record, your cooperation is greatly appreciated."

CHAPTER
TWENTY

AS SOON AS Chief Chambers cleared Alistair's house, he called all the cast and crew to his place for a meeting. Cassidy stuck around to talk to everybody there as well.

Jackson and I hung out. Me, because I was a part of the cast, and Jackson because he was a detective and Cassidy hadn't shooed him away.

There was a murmur in the air as everyone gathered. It seemed that the whole crew was curious about what was going on and knew something was wrong. I stood in the back of the crowd and observed everybody.

I'd learned the skill from Jackson. He was always the one standing on the periphery soaking everything in and looking for trouble. It was a trademark of cops, I supposed. But I found the trait worked well for me also. My natural inclination was to jump into the middle of things. But when there was a potential killer in the room, it paid to have some discretion.

Alistair clapped his hands together, as flamboyant as ever. "Okay, okay, everybody! Thank you all for joining me here."

At his words, everybody found a seat either on the couch, a chair, or the floor. Cassidy stood beside Alistair, almost like a warden, and everyone's eyes were fastened on them.

"As you all might know," Alistair started. "There have been some very strange and suspicious things happening since we began to film this movie. Not only is somebody messing with our script and hacking into my email, but we also have one person who is now dead. This morning someone broke into my place and tied me up."

A gasp sounded throughout the room, followed by a low murmur as people whispered amongst themselves.

Alistair raised his chin dramatically, and I again imagined him doing a dance competition. Perhaps that's what this was for him—a dance. He made a move and then waited for everyone else to follow. He liked taking the lead.

But could he be trusted?

"I have been working with the police to try to

ascertain what is going on in the situation," Alistair said.

I could tell that Alistair was being on his best behavior around the police chief. Normally, he'd be verbally slandering everybody out of frustration over the whole situation. I could hear a *Cante Grande* playing in the background.

He swung his head to the left and then the right. "It appears, though we don't have definite proof, that somebody in this cast and crew might be involved with these crimes."

Another gasp sounded, followed by a new round of murmurs.

I glanced around, looking for anyone who was acting suspiciously. Like maybe somebody who didn't look surprised or shocked. My gaze stopped on Washington George.

He sat by himself, and, instead of turning toward anybody in the room or making eye contact, he stared at Alistair.

Was that because he was trying to maintain a façade and not show he was guilty? I had no idea. But I kept that fact in the back of my mind just in case.

"I've asked you all to come here so we can have an open discussion about what is going on," Alistair continued. "First and foremost, I do not want anyone else in my cast or crew to be injured or threatened. Secondly, I want you to know that if you are the one who was behind messing with my script, I will have you blackballed in Hollywood so fast that—" Alistair cut himself off as his emotions began to rise.

He let out a deep breath, rolled his shoulders back, and cast a quick glance at Cassidy, who gave him a warning look.

"Like I was saying, I don't want to think that anybody involved in the production of this movie could be a part of this. But that is what the evidence is pointing to. Police Chief Cassidy Chambers is here today. She has some questions for all of you."

As he paused, everyone waited, no one daring to say anything. Alistair's gaze met each of ours. When he started again, I could mentally hear a castanet clapping together.

Sometimes, it was the little things that amused me the most, like my mental commentary on this whole situation. Obviously, no one could hear it but me. But I was enough.

"As you well know, we are behind on our filming schedule now, which was already tight, with little room for error," he said. "I'm going to be meeting with my production staff today so we can figure out a revised schedule. I'd appreciate all of your cooperation."

Cassidy stepped forward. "Like Alistair said, I appreciate you all coming here. We're taking this crime very seriously."

"Do you know who killed the pirate?" Sarah asked.

I glanced at her. With her wide eyes and pensive expression, she looked terrified. I suppose this had shaken everybody up more than I'd thought.

"My team is working hard to figure out what happened to the man known as Bucky Belching," Cassidy said. "Right now, we have a few suspects and leads we're investigating, but we do not know anything definite yet. Nobody has been arrested."

"How can you assure us that our safety is paramount here?" Brandon, the gaffer, asked.

"While we want to do everything we can to ensure that you all remain safe, it's of paramount importance that you all take steps yourselves during this time," Cassidy said. "Make sure that you don't go anywhere alone, and use common sense."

That was so much easier said than done sometimes.

"Also, I know this should go without saying, but if you see something, say something," Cassidy continued. "This isn't just true when it comes to terrorism. What happened here is a serious crime, as I'm sure you're all aware. Now, I would like to pull several of you aside individually and talk with you. In the meantime, I would like to ask the rest of you to remain here. Thank you."

Cassidy started by pulling aside Sarah. The police chief was using an office here in the house for privacy purposes. The rest of us continued to wait in the living room.

As soon as she left, everyone began talking. I could feel the fear in the air. It was one thing to act out fake crimes, but it was an entirely different story to have to face the reality of death while on the set.

The optimistic part of myself wanted to think that this film could recover. But the realistic part of me wasn't so sure. Or maybe it was the hopeful part of me. After all, I was already over filming this movie even though the production had just started.

Jackson leaned close. "Hopefully, Cassidy will discover something new."

"We can only hope."

Our gazes fell on somebody across the room. Washington stood, wandered into the kitchen, paced around for a bit, and now headed away from the others.

Jackson leaned closer to me and whispered in my ear, "I'm going to keep an eye on him."

"That's a great idea," I told him. "I'll stay in here and keep an eye on everybody else."

As Jackson walked away, I mentally smiled. It almost sounded like Jackson and I were a team. I mean, we *were* a team. But it sounded like we were almost an *official* team.

And that made me happy.

Usually I just felt like I got in the way of his investigations, but since he wasn't officially investigating —and neither was I—we could both unofficially investigate together. It was a twisted logic, but logic was still logic.

He disappeared around the corner following after Washington George. I wondered where my costar was going and why he was acting so strange. I didn't know much about the man, only that he'd done a couple of films that had done fairly well, and he was known as a rising star within the Hollywood circles I was in.

He was certainly handsome enough, and he could have charisma. And what I meant by that was that he could also be moody at times. I supposed that was typical of the creative temperament. There were highs and lows.

But ever since I came to Lantern Beach, Washington seemed to be on the low end of that spectrum. Was that because he was up to something? I had no idea.

"So, this is all crazy, isn't it?" Mindy sidled up next to me.

"I know," I said. "I just can't believe it. It seems like it should happen in a movie, but not in real life."

"You really think someone here on the crew is guilty?"

"I suppose that's what it all points to. We just need to find a connection with someone here to the pirate who died. You don't know anything about that, do you?"

"I did see Eva out the other night," Mindy said.

There Mindy went again, throwing Eva under the bus, so to speak. Was that because Eva really was guilty? Or was there a deeper motivation here? I needed to find out more information.

"Where did you see Eva?"

"I went to this restaurant on the boardwalk after filming was finished the first night. There weren't many places that are open late, but this one—The Docks—was one of them. Eva was there. You know she's the life of the party and loves to be the center of attention."

"So what happened?" I crossed my arms, anxious to hear what she had to say.

"Some guys were hitting on her. I mean, what's new with that, right? But some of those pirates from the cosplay gathering were also there. They were flirting with her, and she was flirting back. In fact, they started singing pirate songs and dancing on tables. I thought that someone was going to call the police."

I stored that new information away. It was very interesting.

"So was the dead man one of the men she was flirting with?"

"No, he wasn't," Mindy said. "But there was this other pirate who was especially . . . how do you say it? Aggressive, I suppose. He and Eva were all over each other."

"Is that right?" My mind raced through the various pirates I'd seen that day on the beach, acting out their fake little battles.

"Surprisingly enough, I actually did hear his name," Mindy continued. "Or, at least, I heard his stage name. I can't imagine it would be his real name."

My pulse quickened. "And what was it?"

"Corky Keelhauler."

I was mulling over Mindy's words. It looked like things were pointing back to Eva again. But what about what Eva said earlier?

She'd seemed genuinely shaken about everything that was going on. Did that imply that she wasn't guilty? Or could she be guilty but still shaken?

What if she sent herself flowers and the threatening note just to throw suspicion off of herself? I supposed that was possible.

Just thinking about everything was giving me a headache, though.

In the meantime, I glanced around, wondering where Jackson was. He'd disappeared fifteen minutes ago.

As a thought entered my mind, a shot of fear followed. I didn't want to be paranoid, but on the other hand, I had seen a lot of bad things happen. What if Jackson had been following Washington George and something had happened to him?

I started toward the hallway where Jackson had disappeared. But, before I could walk down it, Jackson came around the corner. He took my elbow and led me away from the rest of the crowd and into the kitchen where no one else was gathered at the moment.

Before he could say anything, the door to the office opened, and Sarah and Cassidy stepped out. Cassidy called Mindy into the office to talk to her.

I had told Mindy that she needed to tell Cassidy exactly what she had just told me. Maybe Cassidy could make sense of things. I'd like to step up to the plate but . . . chasing down pirates wasn't on my agenda.

My first priority was filming. My second priority was Jackson.

If circumstances were different, I might have tried to track down some of these guys myself. But that wasn't going to happen.

As soon as Cassidy disappeared, Jackson lowered his voice.

"It's not Washington," he said. "At least, I don't think it is. I'll need to verify his story, of course."

"What story?" The man had a tendency to drink and fly off the handle. He seemed like a good suspect to me.

"He's a recovering alcoholic," Jackson said. "Whenever he gets stressed, he fights the urge to drink. He just had to make a call to his sponsor because he doesn't want to get derailed."

"That's why he looked so frazzled . . ." It suddenly made sense.

"And get this—someone left a six pack of beer outside his room the other night."

"What? Why would someone do that? It's almost like they want him to fail."

"Exactly. And the night Bucky died? Washington was participating in an online support group. Apparently, six different people can testify he was there, talking through his issues. Most of it was through video."

Well . . . there went that lead.

Who else did that leave?

CHAPTER
TWENTY-ONE

AFTER CASSIDY HAD FINISHED INTERVIEWING everybody, she gathered her notes and turned to me and Jackson. She motioned for us to walk with her away from any listening ears.

"Thank you for all your help so far." Her voice was low so no one else could hear. "I'm going to go back to the station and review everything I've learned."

"Did you find out anything helpful?" I desperately hoped all of this hadn't been for nothing.

"Not particularly." Cassidy frowned and glanced at the people in the distance. "But there were a few comments I want to look into a little bit further."

"Mindy told you about seeing Eva at that restaurant hanging out with some pirates a couple nights ago, right?" I asked, hoping she'd carried through with her promise.

"Yes, she did," Cassidy said. "I plan on looking into that as well. Although I've already talked to this Corky Keelhauler, I'm going to dig a little deeper and make sure that his alibi can be verified. There's one other thing I wanted to mention."

"What's that?" Jackson asked.

"One of my guys found a treasure map today. Maybe the one the pirate group used when they charged onto the set.

My pulse quickened. "Okay . . ."

"It was in the woods near the lighthouse," Cassidy said. "One of these pirates was hanging around a little more than they've owned up to. We're checking for fingerprints and everything else. I just thought I'd let you know."

"Thank you," Jackson said.

"In the meantime, you two be safe."

"We will," Jackson said.

With a wave, Cassidy left. Jackson and I walked back into the living room in time to hear Alistair dismissing everybody from the meeting. He said that filming would resume in the morning, rain or shine.

He also reminded everybody that he would not be sending out any new scripts. And, as a final word, he said if nobody had heard from him by the time filming was supposed to start, to please send someone to check on him.

Before I left, I slipped into his bathroom for a moment. When I couldn't find a towel to dry my hands, I opened one of the drawers there.

A pink sweater was folded inside.

A pink sweater?

I pulled it out and studied the clothing a minute. The cardigan looked familiar. Where had I seen it before?

I didn't know.

I quickly folded it again and placed it back in the cabinet.

A few minutes later, Jackson and I were in his truck. I told him about the sweater as we sat in the driveway a moment.

It had been a long day, and darkness was already falling outside. I had a house full of people waiting for me so this might be our only chance to talk alone.

I turned to him. "Okay, help me out here. This is what we know so far. Whoever's behind this is sending out new scripts every day. In order to do this, they've had to somehow mirror Alistair's email account. To me, that means they have to have more than a basic grasp of technology and computers."

"Agreed."

"They also sent a note to the man known as Bucky Belching, threatening to kill him."

"Whether or not it was threatening is not in question," Jackson said. "It said he was a target."

"Sounds threatening to me. And someone did kill him. Either Bucky or the killer left a note in his pocket with my name on it and some random numbers."

Jackson stretched his arm across the back of the seat. "Bucky could've written that himself, intending to give it to you."

"You mean, maybe he came to the set to leave that note for me, but, in the process, something happened to him?"

"I think that's a good possibility," Jackson said. "Maybe this Bucky guy was never the target at all. Maybe he was in the wrong place at the wrong time."

That seemed like a good theory but . . . "That still doesn't explain the threatening note he got."

Jackson pressed his lips together before saying, "What did it say again? Heed my warning or you will die."

"That sounds right."

"Whoever this person is, they also tied up Alistair, and they threatened Eva." Jackson ran a hand over his face, looking both tired and invigorated. "I think one other thing we need to look at in order to find this person is motive. Why would somebody be doing this? That's what I don't quite understand. Every time I think I have a suspect, there are pieces that don't fit."

I couldn't agree more. "It could be someone who hates Alistair and wants to ruin his movie. I mean, altering the script, having a dead body on the set, and tying him up . . . to me that all points to him being the target."

"If what you said is right, then we're looking for somebody who has a vendetta against Alistair." Jackson's gaze fell on me. "Any idea who that might be?"

"It could be any number of people, I suppose. Alistair doesn't have the most charming personality. I'm sure he has mistreated people in his effort to get to the top. Most of the cast and crew don't especially feel loyalty to him, but he is a great manipulator. He is one of these 'I'll scratch your back if you scratch mine' type of people. Who knows how many people are here just because he has maybe promised them favors?"

"It's not that I want you to look into this, but just keep your eyes open for anybody who might seem to have a grudge against him." Jackson's gaze latched onto mine, and I could see the concern there. Somebody wasn't playing games here, and Bucky had paid the price.

"Don't worry. I'll definitely be keeping my eyes open—both for my own safety, as well as just out of plain curiosity."

"At least we can rule Washington George out," Jackson said.

"And then there is Eva," I said. "Mindy told me that she saw Eva at a local restaurant with some pirates, one of those pirates being Corky Keelhauler."

"Let's think this through for a moment." Jackson pressed his lips together and stared out the window. "Is there any possibility that none of this actually has to do with the movie? Could this crime be totally unrelated to the movie, but just happen to be happening on the side?"

I wanted to believe that but . . . "I don't see how that's possible. If it's not related to the movie, then why is someone playing with the script?"

"What if somebody heard the script had been altered the day before, so they left a dead body the next day to throw suspicion off them?"

His words washed over me. He could be onto something.

"There is a possibility that somebody went out that night after filming and started running their mouth, especially if they had some alcohol in them," I said. "I could see one of the cast or crew members telling some locals what happened. Maybe the killer just happened to be near and saw it as an opportunity to get rid of Bucky."

"But if that was the case then why did Alistair get tied up? Why is someone sending you threatening texts? Sending Eva dead roses?"

I let out a long breath. "Those are great questions. I don't have any great answers. In fact, my head is starting to pound. Nothing is really making sense. If we had to pick a direction to go with this case, where should that even be?"

"I have to say," Jackson said. "I don't really know. What I do know is that we're not investigating, and that Cassidy and her officers are on top of this."

"What about Eva?"

"Cassidy is going to station someone at her place tonight."

"That's good to know."

"Even though I'm not officially involved, I do want to keep my eyes open. The best thing that we can do until we have more answers is to be aware of everything happening around us."

"I agree. Hopefully, Cassidy is getting more answers than we are."

I really hoped so. Especially when I remembered that picture of myself . . . the dead woman.

Just as the thought entered into my head, Jackson's phone dinged. He squinted as he clicked on something.

I could tell by the way his shoulder tensed that something was wrong. "What is it?"

He showed me his screen. "Someone has been filming us."

I watched a video there. It was of Jackson and me sitting in his truck . . . in the driveway . . . from just a few minutes ago.

My lungs tightened.

I glanced around but saw no one. Only sand dunes, a dark lane, and a soggy rain.

"It looks like it was shot from over there." Jackson pointed to a sand dune in the distance, his voice hardening. "Stay here."

And then he climbed from his truck and stormed toward that very area.

As much as I wanted to stay in the truck, there was no way I was staying here while Jackson was out there chasing bad guys.

I stepped onto the driveway and glanced in the direction he'd gone. It was dark outside now, and it was hard to see anything. Rain slithered down my cheeks and dampened my clothes.

I heard a footfall in the distance, and I gasped.

Was it the killer?

I shrank back against the truck.

As I did, Jackson emerged from the beach, a shadowy look on his face.

"Did you catch him?" I asked.

He shook his head. "No, he's gone. But I don't like this."

"I don't like it either."

We climbed back into his truck and slammed the doors. A few seconds later, Jackson and I started back to my place.

"How did someone get your number?" I asked.

"Good question. I suppose someone could have seen you dialing it. Maybe this is someone I gave my card to. Who knows?"

This day seemed to be lasting a week. Too much had happened. Too much bad stuff.

I was excited to see the gang. I really was. I was thrilled that they had taken time out of their schedule to come here to Lantern Beach and to spend time with me and Jackson.

But . . . I'd be lying if I didn't say there another part of me that was tired. A lot had happened since I had arrived in town, and the stress of filming this movie was starting to get to me. Plus, there was the fact that I really needed some alone time with Jackson. It was going to be hard to get that when I had six extra guests in my home.

But I wasn't complaining. I really wasn't.

As Jackson pulled up to my house, he put his truck in Park and cut the engine. The rain had started to come down harder, pitter-pattering on the top of his truck. Both of us sat there for a moment, not saying anything.

Jackson reached over, grabbed my hand, and squeezed it. I squeezed back. I missed the simple times just like this. The times where we didn't really have to say anything but we could just be together.

Was what Phoebe had said true? Was Jackson sad?

That thought did something to my heart. It made it twist and ache in all kinds of ways that I didn't like.

"You think any more about that wedding date?" Jackson asked.

As soon as the words hit my ears, my shoulders tensed and any laid-back feelings disappeared. Why did this feel so stressful to me? It didn't make any sense.

"I'm still thinking that early May might be the best time," I said. "I think we should just nail down a date, and I'm going to make everything else work around it."

Jackson turned to me. "I just want to make sure that your schedule is clear before we start looking at locations and booking things. I know how quickly things can get out of control."

I wanted to deny the truth in his words, but I couldn't. He was correct. It was so easy for my schedule to control me instead of me controlling my schedule.

"Okay, here's what I'll do. I will talk to my producer and make sure that date is clear. Not that I need his permission, but I also do not want any miscommunication to mess things up or to make things stressful and take away from the beauty of our big day."

"And you still want to get married in Nags Head, correct?"

"That's right. A beach wedding. I think it'll be the perfect place."

"But you also know if we do it in a place like that there could be paparazzi," Jackson said. "There's a chance that word will leak about when and where our wedding is."

At his words, I frowned. I knew they were true, and I hadn't been in denial about that. But hearing them out loud made my stomach twist. I did not want the paparazzi involved in our wedding.

"I can have everybody we hire sign a nondisclosure agreement," I said. "People in Hollywood do that all the time."

"Despite those nondisclosure agreements, word still leaks." Jackson leveled his gaze with me. "You know it's true, right?"

"Yes, that's true." I sighed and felt my shoulders droop.

I didn't want anything to mess up our big day. I already had one failed marriage, and, even though my ex-spouse had been abusive, I still carried the weight of those decisions. Failed relationships were never easy.

When you were married, that person became a part of you. Even when you weren't together anymore, there was still an emotional impact present.

That was why I wanted to do everything I could to ensure that things with Jackson wouldn't go that route. I wanted to make sure our big day was perfect. But not only that. I didn't want to put all my efforts into the wedding and none of my efforts into the marriage. There was so much to balance, and so much to think about.

Jackson squeezed my hand again and nudged my chin up. "Hey. I'm not trying to be a downer. I just want everything to go the way you want it to go, with no mess-ups. I just want you to be happy."

I felt a smile begin at the edge of my lips. "Being with you makes me happy."

"Well, I am glad to hear that because being with you makes me happy too." He leaned closer and planted a kiss on my lips.

It lingered for a moment, and I felt myself melting. This was just what I needed. I needed something that would help me forget everything else was going on right now. Jackson was the perfect medicine for that.

We pulled away, and Jackson ran his hand down my face before kissing my forehead.

"We should get inside," he murmured.

"Yes, I suppose we should."

It sounded like the rain had let up for a minute, so Jackson and I both ran from the truck, up the stairs, and to the front door of the home. We paused there for a moment. Before I could punch in the code to my front door, I heard a foot fall behind me.

The next instant Jackson had his gun drawn. He aimed it at a shadowy figure that had stepped behind me.

CHAPTER
TWENTY-TWO

I SUCKED in a breath as a figure came into view.

It was Corky Keelhauler.

I recognized him from the picture Cassidy had shown me. He was tall and lanky, with greasy hair he wore pulled back in a low ponytail. Like all the other pirates in town, he wore his pirate costume and talked with a slightly British accent.

As soon as he saw Jackson's gun, he raised his hands in the air. "Please, I'm not here to start trouble. I just want to talk."

Jackson eyed him skeptically. "How did you find us?"

"Everybody here on the island knows where you're staying. It's common knowledge."

I wanted to argue, but, since I'd already heard

that factoid a couple other times, I decided that maybe I shouldn't.

"What are you doing here, Corky?" Jackson's voice sounded hard and left no room for argument.

Corky raised his hands in the air. "Like I said, I just want to talk. I know how all of this works. I know that I look guilty. But I'm not. I did not kill Bucky."

"What happened to him?" Jackson asked. "We heard that the two of you didn't get along very well."

"That's true. We didn't see eye to eye. That doesn't mean that I killed him."

Jackson lowered his gun and put it back in his harness. But his face clearly said he was still perturbed. "What exactly were you arguing about?"

"Simple. We were arguing over Gypsy Queen."

"What is Gypsy Queen?" I asked, expecting it to be a new rock band or something. "Is she friends with the 'Dancing Queen' by chance?"

"What? You mean, *who*. She is fairest of all the fairest maidens in the land. Fairer than even you, dare I say?"

I almost wanted to be insulted. Then again, who was I to feel slighted by somebody who is named Gypsy Queen? Either way, I was now mentally singing the Abba song, and I was sure it would be stuck in my head for the rest of the night.

"And why were you arguing over Gypsy Queen?" Jackson asked.

"Because we were both in love with her."

Jackson let out a quick sigh, looking like he was moderating a middle school debate. "And who was Gypsy Queen in love with?"

A frown crossed Corky's face. "Bucky. He won. His commitment to the pirate life greatly impressed her."

I supposed we all had our things that impressed us about the opposite sex. I couldn't ever say for myself that the pirate life was what impressed me, but to each his own.

"Where is this Gypsy Queen now?" Jackson asked.

Corky's face darkened. "She left. Said she was walking away from this life. I secretly suspect that her job as an attorney became demanding and her colleagues gave her a hard time."

We both stared at him until he shrugged.

"What? It's true. Even people like lawyers some-times have an inner freak just waiting to let loose."

Jackson cleared his throat. "So you're saying that the only reason you two had been arguing was because of Gypsy?"

"That's right. It was our only disagreement. I do

agree that it was a heated one. However, I met another fair maiden. A gal named Eva."

I blinked, remembering Mindy's story. "Eva? Where did the two of you meet?"

"At a restaurant called The Docks two nights ago. We talked until morning."

I glanced at Jackson. It looked like Eva might have an alibi for that night, after all.

"Did you threaten to shoot Bucky?" Jackson asked. "Someone overheard something like that the night the two of you were arguing."

"I think I tuned him out at that point. Maybe he said something like 'this was his last shot' or something? It didn't seem significant."

"Is there anybody else you know who didn't get along with Bucky?" Jackson asked. "Anyone who might want him dead?"

Corky looked from side to side, as if he thought someone might be listening. "There was this one man that Bucky didn't like. He's only known as the Piranha."

Man, these names were killing me. Part of me loved them. Part of me felt like I'd stepped into a James Bond movie and Kissy Suzuki or Christmas Jones would appear next.

Jackson stepped closer and lowered his voice. "What's this Piranha guy's real name?"

Corky's voice, on the other hand, climbed higher. "I don't know."

"Have you ever seen his face?" I asked. "Does he have any distinguishing features?"

"He operates under a cloak of darkness. He only meets at night, and he wears a black cloak and matching mask."

Jackson let out another small sigh. "We're not getting very far, and I'm losing my patience."

"Why did the Piranha have a problem with Bucky?" I asked, trying to get more answers from this guy before he decided to stop talking.

"I heard he tried to pay Bucky to shoot somebody."

"Bucky was a hitman?" The words left my lips before I could stop them.

"That's what I heard," Corky said. "Bucky never talked about it, though."

"So you're saying that there's a Piranha guy who was trying to pay Bucky to do a hit job?" Jackson's voice rang with disbelief.

Corky shrugged. "I have no idea. I am just telling you what the rumors are."

"Do you know who the target was?" Jackson asked.

Corky's gaze fell on me. "Joey Darling, of course."

Jackson and I exchanged a look. This whole thing was just getting weirder and weirder by the minute.

Corky left, and Jackson and I stepped into my house. Part of me hoped that everybody was already in bed because that was all that I wanted too. I had a lot to process.

But, instead, as soon as I walked into the living room, I was bushwhacked.

No, not bushwhacked. I glanced around.

People had thrown me a . . . party?

I glanced at Jackson. His hand was on his gun. Didn't people know better than to surprise a detective?

I suppose they didn't. All of my concerns washed away when I realized what was happening.

My friends were throwing me a surprise bridal shower.

I glanced around and saw their smiling faces and eyes that beamed with pride. They had gone through a lot of work to plan and organize this to surprise us. There were balloons tied in various places and a table full of presents, cake, and other treats to eat.

And right now everyone stood around staring at me and Jackson.

"We just couldn't wait any longer to celebrate your upcoming marriage," Dizzy said. "We are just so excited for you. We came here just to do the shower."

Tears rushed my eyes. I didn't know what to say.

It still amazed me when people did sweet things for me. Usually when people were nice to me it was because they wanted something. I'd never had a lot of great friendships with other women, and many of the ones I did have had ended poorly.

The fact that someone—several someones—had gone out of their way to do all this for me and Jackson? It touched my heart in more ways than I could express.

Jackson seemed to sense my emotional state, and his arm went to my waist. He squeezed. I looked up, and we exchanged a smile.

"You guys . . . you shouldn't have. But I love this, and I am so thrilled," I told them. "Thank you all so much."

A round of hugs were exchanged with all of them.

The next couple hours were spent opening gifts, talking, eating, laughing, and eating some more.

It was the perfect ending to an otherwise not-so-perfect day.

I was so glad my friends had come. I was so glad

to have them in my life. To have people who cared about me enough to do something like this.

Now I really needed to nail down that wedding date.

CHAPTER
TWENTY-THREE

"OKAY, OKAY, EVERYONE," Alistair yelled, dramatically swinging his head around.

I could mentally hear the mariachi music playing.

He'd gathered us near the production trailer the next morning, bright and early. I was already dressed in my Drusilla costume and ready for today's filming. Unfortunately, someone had broken into Mindy's trailer last night and cut the tips off all her makeup brushes.

After a few tears, she'd improvised using her fingers and Q-tips.

We'd called Cassidy—again. She'd questioned Larry, but he hadn't seen anything—of course. That would have been too easy.

Apparently, everything that had happened had pushed Alistair into fast gear, because he looked all business right now. Everyone seemed to have bated breath as we waited to hear what he was going to tell us.

He paced, his poofy hair blowing with the breeze. "As you all know we have had some setbacks on the filming of this movie. Also, as you all know, Joey Darling only has two weeks to film this movie in between shooting everything else that she is involved with."

You had to be kidding me. He was throwing me under the bus again? Now *my* knickers were getting in a knot.

"Because of circumstances out of our control, we are going to have to rearrange filming some of these scenes," Alistair continued. "Joey is not in every scene, so we will be filming out of order. I know this isn't ideal, and it's not how I like to organically film my movies. However, this is the way it's going to have to be done. So, from here on out we'll be filming Joey's scenes until they are completed, and then we will film the rest of the movie." Alistair's gaze scanned everybody else's. "Does everybody understand what I'm saying?"

A round of murmurs went around the space, and everyone nodded.

Alistair clapped his hands, and more Spanish music began playing in my mind. "All right, everyone. We don't have any time to waste, so let's get started."

I glanced at Jackson. He stood near the cameras, out of sight, and out of the way. But I knew he was watching and listening to everything that Alistair said. He was clearly still worried about everything going on.

I trudged toward the filming area, my thoughts still churning.

At this point, I felt like Eva could be cleared from any possible involvement in this crime. I also felt like Washington George was cleared. Now we just needed to figure out who the Piranha was. Whoever this man turned out to be, I felt certain he had some answers.

As we prepared to start the scene, I glanced around. Speaking of Eva, where was she? Was she running late? It was a possibility. But what if it was something more sinister?

A bad feeling started to grow in my gut. I knew I wasn't going to be able to let this pass. I had to say something. What if something had happened to Eva?

Even though Cassidy had someone watching her, that didn't mean Eva was okay. I'd filmed enough episodes of *Relentless* to know how clever bad guys could be—after all, even the fictitious ones were created in the minds of real people.

Just as Alistair was about to yell "action," I raised my hands in a T sign and yelled, "Cut!"

I ignored everyone's dirty looks. I'd already messed up the production schedule, and now I was messing it up more.

"Has anybody seen Eva?" I asked.

Everybody glanced around at each other and shrugged. I knew what that meant. It meant that nobody had seen her and no one knew where she was.

My gaze met Jackson's. This wasn't good. It wasn't good at all.

Jackson volunteered to help search for Eva. Reluctantly, he'd left me on set with some very specific instructions about staying put until he came back, keeping my eyes open for trouble, and not running upstairs when confronted by a deadly killer.

He hadn't worded it exactly that way, but that's what he meant.

I, of course, wanted to help find Eva also, but Alistair didn't seem to be on board with that. He insisted that she was probably fine. That she could be a diva. That she'd probably overslept because she had been out the night before partying again.

He hadn't looked happy as he had shared any of that, but I couldn't deny the truth of his statements. She did like to party, she was chronically late, and she did have diva-like tendencies. But the bad feeling remained in my gut.

Even as I delivered my lines and acted out my scenes, all I could think about was Eva and all the bad things that might have happened. I hoped and prayed that Eva was okay and had not become another victim.

Two hours later, we took a break from filming. We'd actually made quite a bit of progress. But I was concerned because Jackson still wasn't back, nor had I been able to talk to him to see what he'd found out.

We had fifteen minutes while they set up the next scene. I decided to go to my trailer to call Jackson. I walked inside and headed toward my kitchen table, where I'd left my cell earlier.

But my table was empty. My phone wasn't there.

How could that be possible? I'd left it right here.

My throat tightened. I glanced around the space. Had someone been in here again?

Even worse—were they still here?

My gaze darted around. Nothing else appeared to be touched.

Just to be safe, I checked behind the doors.

Nothing. No one.

Still, the bad feeling grew in my gut.

As I sat down to think this through, I saw something sticking out from the cushions of my couch. My phone! I picked it up and hit the screen button.

Nothing seemed different. But I felt confident I hadn't left the device there.

Out of curiosity, I pulled up my photos. I gasped at what I saw.

Someone had handled my phone. And they'd left a photo. It was taken from the window of my trailer. I could see everyone outside filming.

Someone had wanted to send me a message—a message that they were close and accessible.

A shiver shimmied down my spine.

Before I could figure out my next move, a knock sounded at my door. I peered out the window and saw Sarah standing there. Based on her frown, there was more bad news.

I opened the door and let her inside, my shoulders tensing as I waited.

"Joey, did you see this?" Sarah's face looked tight with worry, and she held up something in her hands.

"See what?" I had no idea what she was talking about, and I wasn't sure I wanted to know.

She held up a copy of the *National Instigator*. I physically revolted at what I saw on the cover.

It was a picture of me.

In costume for this movie. On set.

The photo was a doozy. The high definition showed all of my wrinkles and chins and thinning hair and added weight.

"How in the world was that picture leaked?" I ran my hand over my face. "I mean, I did wear the costume out once, but no one should have recognized me. Besides, this was taken on set."

Sarah shrugged. "I have no idea."

"What does the article say? Has Alistair seen this?"

Sarah shrugged again. "I don't know. I came right to you. I don't want to face his wrath. He's already in a rotten mood today."

I took the magazine from her and opened the pages until I found the article that accompanied the photo. I began reading it out loud.

"Joey Darling is taking on a different kind of role," I read. "She's still playing the spy she's often typecast for. But this time she is playing an aging spook who has secluded herself on an isolated island."

I paused and sucked in a deep breath before continuing.

"Joey Darling has shown her acting chops with this new role. She hasn't shied away from doing the hard things and from taking on difficult roles. In fact, her talent shines in this new movie." I looked up at Sarah. "How would someone know this?"

"I know I keep saying this, but I have no idea. I suppose anyone here on the set could have sent this information."

"If they did, Alistair is not going to be happy."

"No, he is not. This movie is so toxic . . ."

Yes, it was.

I glanced at the byline.

Marcus Whiting. I'd never heard of the man before.

I looked out the window and saw Jackson approaching my trailer. I lowered the magazine to my side and opened the door to let him in.

I held my breath as I waited to hear what he had discovered about Eva. Based on his stormy expression, it wasn't good news.

"Well?" I asked, waiting.

"Eva is gone," Jackson said. "We searched her room at the inn. Her personal belongings are still there, but she's not there. She's nowhere to be seen."

The bad feeling in my gut continued to grow. What was going on here? And when would it end?

I didn't know. But I had to tell Jackson about the photo on my phone. And then I needed to share that information with Cassidy.

CHAPTER
TWENTY-FOUR

AN HOUR LATER, we still hadn't begun to film again. Jackson and Cassidy had given Alistair the update, and, as expected, he wasn't happy. I was pretty sure we wouldn't be filming any more today now that Eva was missing.

The fact that she was nowhere to be seen had me worried. This was what had been written and inserted into the script. Vanished . . . then dead. I had been worried that something like this would happen. I prayed she was still alive and unharmed.

A cold shiver went down my spine.

I knew my timing was bad, but, despite that, I cleared my throat and held up the magazine. Alistair, Jackson, and Cassidy were all near as I did so.

Right now, we were all gathered outside my trailer. It was midday, and the sun had decided to heat up everything around us. The sand seemed to absorb the warmth and act as a heater.

My suit didn't make anything better—it acted as an insulator and trapped all the heat.

"I know this may or may not be connected with everything that's been happening," I started. "But this issue of the *National Instigator* came out this morning, and, not only is my picture on the cover, but there is an article about this movie. Does anyone know anything about this?"

Alistair's eyes widened, and he snatched the magazine from me. His eyes bulged as he flipped through the pages. "How in the world did this get out? Who would've done this? We must have a traitor on this set."

"So you think that somebody here on location sold this information to the tabloid?" Cassidy's hands went to her hips and her gaze narrowed.

"It's the only thing that makes sense," Alistair said. "Otherwise, how would this have leaked? We obviously have a spy on our hands."

"I realize you already know this." Jackson stepped forward to address Alistair. "But somehow the script has also gotten out, so if that's possible, then it's also possible that other information has been leaked. But I agree that it does appear that you have somebody on the inside here."

"I hate to believe that anybody I trust, that anybody here in my circle, would be responsible for this." Alistair shook his head, his expression stormy.

"We're going to need to talk to everybody here." Cassidy's voice left no room for argument. Gone was the sweet woman I'd had dinner with, and in her place was a hardcore professional. "It's not a crime that this information has been published, but we need to figure out how all these pieces are connected. We also need to know the last time each of you saw Eva."

Alistair's eyes widened, and he fanned his face. "You think that something may have happened to her? Something other than her disappearing?"

"I think we need to assume the worst-case scenario right now," Cassidy said. "Especially when considering everything else that has happened here on the set."

Alistair scowled and muttered a few things under his breath. He turned away from us, muttered a few more things, and then finally composed himself enough to say, "This movie is never going to finish filming, is it?"

"Of course it is," I said.

Alistair scowled again, still looking put off.

"Listen," Jackson said. "How about if I help? I'll call the *National Instigator* and see if I can find out who this Marcus Whiting person is who supposedly wrote the article."

"That sounds good," Cassidy said. "Let's meet back together later and share what we learn."

I just hoped that later wasn't too late.

After lunch, Jackson and I were in my trailer, each doing our own thing. He was waiting for a call back from the magazine, and I was studying my upcoming scenes. As I reviewed the ending of the film, my spine stiffened.

"What is it?" Jackson glanced over at me from the kitchen table where he sat.

I shook my head, hoping that the conclusions I drew were incorrect. But I'd be foolish if I didn't mention my suspicions here.

"I know this is probably nothing," I started, looking up from my spot on the couch. "But in the original script . . . at the end of the film . . . I die."

Jackson glanced at me. "But that's not new. Still, you think . . ."

I shrugged. "I don't know what to think. This killer seems to hint about what's to come through the revisions he sends out. But knowing I have a death scene at the end still bothers me. Maybe I'm just being paranoid."

He abandoned his spot at the table and came over to sit by me. He draped his arm around the back of the couch, wrinkles forming at the corners of his eyes. "I don't like this, Joey. What if you just call it quits? I know you said you signed a contract, but don't people get out of contracts all the time?"

I sucked on my bottom lip a moment, mulling over his words. "Not without a lawsuit."

"I hate to say it, but I'd almost take a lawsuit over all of this." He let out a long breath and shook his head. "Whoever wrote the article appears to be a big fan of yours."

At his words, my blood felt a little colder. I had a super-stalker fan club that liked to follow my every move. They even had a secret group set up online so they could discuss where I was and what I was doing. It was disturbing.

Many of the people involved were mostly innocent. But all it took was one person who was a little bit off-balance, and my life would be turned upside down again.

Just then Jackson's phone rang. He put it to his ear.

"Yes, yes, this is Detective Jackson Sullivan," Jackson said. "We are investigating some crimes centering around the production of this movie, and we need to know who took these pictures and wrote that article."

I couldn't hear what was being said on the other end of the line, but I really wanted to know. I waited several minutes. It sounded like Jackson was put on hold, and then someone else answered, and then somebody else put him on hold.

Finally, after what seemed like forever, Jackson started talking and explaining the situation again.

As the person on the other end of the line began to talk, Jackson picked up a paper and pencil and began jotting a few things down. I tried to glance over his shoulder to see what he was writing, but his script looked more like chicken scratch.

Finally, he ended the call, and he looked at me. "You'll never believe this."

"What? What is it?"

He held up his phone. "This Marcus Whiting . . . this is what he looks like."

I sucked in a breath. Marcus Whiting looked just like Bucky Belching.

CHAPTER
TWENTY-FIVE

"SO, you're telling me that Bucky Belching, a man who was here for a pirate cosplay event, was also a member of the paparazzi?" Cassidy said, looking back and forth between Jackson and me. She'd come to my trailer so we could share the news with her. "And you're saying that he somehow got on set, took pictures of you, and wrote up this article for the *National Instigator*?"

I nodded, still processing everything myself. "That's how it appears."

I had only a few minutes to talk to her before filming would resume. Alistair had said that, despite everything that happened, the show must go on.

"I talked to the editor-in-chief myself," Jackson said. "She confirmed that Bucky Belching was the person she bought these photos and article from—only he went by a different name, obviously."

"But none of you ever saw him on set?" Cassidy asked.

"He could have been with the mob of pirates who accidentally wandered onto the set the first day of filming." I held up the magazine. "If you look at the angle of these photos, it almost appears they were taken from the distance. I am wondering if he was hiding out in a patch of woods with some type of telephoto lens and that's how he got these shots."

Cassidy pressed her lips together, a focused, intense look in her gaze. "I am surprised that nobody would have noticed him there."

"The woods are pretty thick over there." Jackson nodded out the window, toward the patch of trees Bucky had emerged from that night he approached Jackson and me. "He could have been hiding out over there and taking these."

Cassidy nodded slowly, a hint of doubt in her gaze. "I agree—and it is the same basic area where we found the pirate map. But how would he have known that you were doing a good job unless he was close enough to hear?"

Something about what I'd heard earlier kept probing me. But what was it?

That's how he got these shots . . .

I straightened, realizing exactly what it was. "That argument that Lou overheard Bucky having? What if he was talking about doing a shoot—a photo shoot?"

"Keep going." Cassidy's eyes widened as she processed what I said. "You could be on to something."

"This all makes sense now," Jackson said. "This Bucky guy wasn't a hitman. He was a member of the paparazzi. He wasn't an amateur photographer chasing sunsets, like Lou said. That was just a cover."

"I think you could be right," Cassidy said.

Jackson rubbed his jaw, his eyes still glazed with thought. "Did you find his camera, by chance?"

"No, like I said earlier, I suspect the killer disposed of his things in the ocean."

"What are the chances they'll wash ashore?" I asked.

"Unlikely. But we're keeping our eyes open." Cassidy shifted. "Let's think this through. "If our theory is correct, why did Bucky approach you two with that supposed death threat? How would that fit?"

I leaned back, trying to think it through. The nice thing about being creative was that ideas came naturally to me. Plus, I'd been around enough reporters to know how they think. Why would he make up that threat? It was clearly a message someone had left him about getting some photos.

"The media . . . they can be vultures. My guess is that this Bucky guy used that supposed threat as an excuse to find out more information on me. He was trying to be sneaky by playing on my compulsion to help people."

"I suppose that makes sense." Cassidy frowned, squinting as if deep in thought. "I can't even imagine living the kind of life you do, where everyone thinks they deserve a piece of you."

"It has its challenges." That could be an understatement. "What I'm also wondering is if taking these photos got Bucky killed? Is that why he was at the lighthouse the night that he died—trying to snoop and get some dirt on me or this film?"

"That's what we need to find out," Cassidy said. "I'll take this information and talk to more of the pirates here on the island. Maybe one of them knows something else."

"Any updates on Eva?" I couldn't get her out of my mind. I kept fearing she'd end up dead just as Bucky had. However, I didn't know why somebody would have targeted her. None of this made sense.

"We haven't discovered anything else on Eva." Cassidy took a step toward the door, looking like she was ready to get back to work. "Nobody appears to have seen her. We've checked the cameras on the ferries and down at the harbor. Nothing. But people just don't disappear off the face of the earth. We'll find out something. Just give us time."

"I'm always available to help if you need me," Jackson said.

I had to admit I was kind of impressed. I knew when Jackson came here, he was looking forward to having some time off, but, apparently, he couldn't resist seeking out a bad guy or helping someone in distress either.

I could understand what that was like. There was a part of me that would much rather be helping to find the bad guy and searching for Eva than filming this movie. Once it got in your blood, it was hard to separate yourself.

Cassidy stood and gathered her things. "I'm going to go and continue to look. Jackson, I think you may best serve by staying here to keep an eye on Joey."

Jackson didn't argue. "I'm inclined to agree. Until we know what's going on, we can't let our guard down. We still don't know who the intended target here is. The entire cast and crew? Is it the film? Until we have those answers, we all need to be careful."

"I'll keep you guys updated if I learn anything," Cassidy said. "And please be careful. We don't need anything else happening here on this island. I just want everyone to be safe."

I could appreciate that sentiment.

As soon as Cassidy left, I turned to Jackson. "There's never a dull moment, is there?"

He rubbed my arms and gazed into my eyes. "There's never a dull moment with you, Joey Darling."

There was something about the way he said those words that caused me to pause. "Does that make you have second thoughts? I mean, your job is already exciting. Maybe you want to come home to peace and quiet."

The words left a sick feeling in my stomach. I'd always assumed that our schedules and lifestyles would eventually mesh. But what if it wasn't the case? What if Jackson was beginning to realize the truth about life with an actress?

He pulled me into his embrace. "You know that's not true, Joey. I just don't understand why trouble always seems to follow you."

"I don't either. This time I'm totally innocent. I did not do anything to provoke these things to happen."

"No, you didn't. I just want to know that you're going to be safe." He kissed the top of my head and held me tighter.

I knew he cared about me and that he was worried. As he should be. It was obvious that whoever was behind these crimes was cold-hearted and escalating. There was still so much I didn't understand.

Even though I had ruled out a couple suspects, that didn't mean I had any new suspects to really take their place. That wasn't comforting. I didn't know who I should be keeping my eyes open for.

Finally, Jackson straightened and pulled back. As much as I would like to stay here in my trailer all day enjoying Jackson's company, I knew that I had to do the job that I was being paid for.

I let out a long breath before saying, "I guess I should get out there."

Jackson seemed to reluctantly let me go. "Yeah, I guess you should."

With Jackson by my side, I wandered from my trailer to the set.

I glanced around and saw Mindy talking to Washington George. I saw Rick setting up his camera in the distance and muttering something to Brandon, probably discussing how to get the perfect angle and sound quality. The one person I didn't see was Alistair.

I really felt like I should talk to him so we could make sure we were on the same wavelength going forward. I had to film this scene and the death one. Then I was done.

"I'm going to see if Alistair is still in his trailer," I told Jackson.

"I'll go with you."

He followed behind me as I walked across the sand, headed that way. At Alistair's door, I knocked. There was no answer.

"Strange," I said. "If he's not in his trailer, where is he?"

"Maybe knock one more time in case he was in the bathroom," Jackson said.

I did as he suggested. I knocked harder and louder. And as I did, the door popped open.

I glanced at Jackson. If he wasn't with me, I wouldn't think twice about pushing the door open and stepping inside. But since he was constantly warning me to stay out of other people's business, I had a moment of pause.

Jackson gave me a little nod, followed by a raised finger telling me to wait. A thrill of delight went up my spine. He had just given me permission to go inside someone else's trailer. I couldn't tell you how happy that made me.

Jackson pulled out his gun and nudged himself in front of me.

That was when I realized what he was thinking— there could be trouble inside.

My gut tightened. What if Alistair was inside? What if he was hurt? Or worse. What if he was dead?

I could hardly stand the thought. Certainly, that wasn't going to happen. Certainly, someone wasn't going to take it that far. But, even as I tried to comfort myself with those reassurances, I knew that they very well could not be certain.

"Hello?" Jackson stepped farther into the space.

I froze and listened. But I heard nothing. There were no footfalls, no music, no murmuring voices. It was like no one was here.

If Alistair wasn't here, then where would he be?

Cautiously, I stepped inside behind Jackson, and my gaze scanned the place. I didn't see anything out of the ordinary. There was still the jackalope, the lava lamp, the leopard-print pillows.

"Hello?" Jackson called out again.

There was still no answer.

I stepped farther inside, my gaze still surveying everything around me. Alistair did not appear to be here, nor did I see any signs of distress. That was good news, I supposed.

I paused by his dresser and looked at a script there. *A Pirate's Life* was the title.

Weird. In the section where there should be an author listed, it was blank.

Was this Alistair's next movie?

Jackson opened one of the doors in the distance, I assumed to make sure that Alistair wasn't hiding out in the space or in trouble. It appeared to be a closet.

But what I saw inside caused me to blanch.

It was a pirate costume. One that included a black cloak and mask.

"A pirate costume?" I mumbled aloud.

Jackson looked at me, and I could tell by his gaze that he was thinking the same thing I was.

I thought I knew exactly who the Piranha was.

It was Alistair.

He must have worn that costume when he met with Bucky. He had access to this location, giving the opportunity and means.

But what about motive? Why in the world would Alistair try to sabotage his own movie? That's what didn't make sense.

CHAPTER
TWENTY-SIX

"WHAT ARE YOU DOING IN HERE?"

Jackson and I turned to see Alistair standing behind us, staring at us with accusation in his gaze.

"The bigger question is, what are you doing with this pirate costume?" Jackson asked.

Alistair's eyes widened. "You're going through my things?"

"We were actually looking for you, afraid that something might have happened and that you were the next victim." I stared at the producer. "But maybe the better question would be what have you done to everyone else?"

Alistair gasped and took a step back. "Do you think I am the one behind this? Why would I sabotage my own movie?"

"That's a great question," Jackson said. "Why would you go to such extreme measures?"

Alistair shook his hand in the air, his breaths seeming to come faster. "You've got this all wrong. I would never kill anybody."

"Then maybe you need to start explaining," I said. "Because that's exactly what it looks like could have happened."

My only comfort right now was in knowing that Jackson had his gun drawn. We should be safe. At least, for the moment.

"Okay, okay." Alistair raised his hands in the air, still staring at Jackson's gun. "I think we all just need to slow down a little bit. Yes, I do have a pirate costume in my closet. But that does not mean that I am behind these crimes."

"Sit down." Jackson pointed to the couch with his gun.

Alistair's gaze remained on Jackson's gun, and he did exactly what Jackson told him to do. Only the overly confident producer wasn't looking so confident right now.

"You're the Piranha, aren't you?" Jackson said.

I crossed my arms, listening carefully to everything Alistair had to say. I was a little more than curious to know what was going on here.

" I . . ." Alistair paused and rubbed his head as if

battling within himself. "Okay, yes. I am the Piranha."

I didn't even bother to hold back my gasp. "So you were the one who commissioned those photographs of me?"

He ran a hand through his hair again, leaving it a frizzy mess. "Yes, okay? It was me."

"Why in the world would you do something like this?" Jackson asked.

Alistair glanced at me, his gaze narrowing. "I was the one that got everything started for you, Joey Darling. And now look at you. You're bigger than I am. You've gone on and made this great name for yourself. You've had setback after setback, yet you've still risen above it all."

"What does this have to do with what's happening here on the set?" I asked. It still didn't make sense.

"I wrote and I am producing this film just for you, Joey. I wanted a role that would humiliate you."

My bottom lip dropped open. "Wait, you created Drusilla Fairweather just to make me look bad?"

Alistair scowled. "Yes, that's correct. Do you feel better now?"

"Do *I* feel better?" I wanted to shriek the words, but I didn't. "Why in the world would that make me feel better?"

"Because you're on to me. You have again proven that you are smarter and more talented than I am."

"Let's take a few steps back here," Jackson said. "You said you wrote this film just to embarrass Joey? Wouldn't making Joey look bad only prove to make you look bad also?"

"No, you don't understand. I was willing to take that risk." Alistair's nostrils flared. "I could make Joey look bad and still have my film be a commercial success. People love these kinds of roles where they see their favorite actors and actresses looking like real people. But there's one thing I didn't foresee happening."

I crossed my arms as bitterness welled inside me. "Like what?"

Alistair's scowl deepened. "I didn't expect for this article to come out giving you praise for doing such a good job in this role. My whole plan is going to be ruined now."

That was just pathetic. I said nothing. What else was there to say?

"So you called yourself the Piranha, disguised yourself as a pirate, and you approached this Bucky Belching—or Marcus Whiting, I should say," Jackson said.

Alistair's jaw flexed. "Yes, that's correct. I'd had a couple encounters with Bucky before. I knew he was involved with this pirate community. I told him he should bring his group here, that I'd help sponsor the event."

"But Bucky didn't know that you were the Piranha, did he?" I asked, trying to form a mental picture of what had happened.

"No, he didn't. I just told him that I needed to get some shots and I gave him the name of a contact at the *National Instigator*. He must have decided to do this professional review himself." He said the word "professional" like it made him want to vomit.

"And then you killed him," Jackson said.

Alistair nearly jumped out of his seat. But when he saw Jackson's gun, he scooted back down. "No, like I said, I would never kill somebody. I have no idea who did that."

"Are you the one who's been sending these revised scripts?" I asked. "They came from your email. You had access to the script."

"No! Why would I?"

"If you would go as far as to try to ruin one of your actresses, I wouldn't put that past you either." Jackson pressed his lips together, obviously unimpressed with Alistair's juvenile actions.

"Look," Alistair said, sweat sprinkled across his forehead. "I know how this appears. I know that I look guilty. That's why I was going to fire Bucky. I was going to call all of this off. But then it was too late."

Jackson stepped closer and nearly growled as he asked, "Where is Eva?"

Alistair's cheeks reddened. "I have no idea what happened to her. I am not behind her disappearance. That's the truth."

"Well, there's one more person you're going to have to tell this to." Jackson shook his head, disgust dripping from his gaze. "The police chief."

I'd wanted to have a Scooby Doo moment, when the bad guy would own up to everything and explain exactly why he did what he did and how. The final reveal looked so natural when it happened on TV. But, in real life, the moment didn't appear to be that easy.

Until Cassidy could get more of the answers she needed, she'd taken Alistair to the police station. As he'd been hauled off the set, he'd screamed at all of us.

First, he'd claimed his innocence. He'd claimed he would prove he was not behind this. Then he'd yelled at everyone listening that filming should continue without him, that time was money, and that they could not afford to shut down production on the set.

I had no idea if he was really guilty or not, but I hoped that Cassidy might get some answers. However, the one thing I didn't understand was how Alistair had tied himself up at the house. Was that even possible? I wasn't sure.

I was going to leave it to the police chief to find these answers. However, I was still thinking about Eva.

I assumed Cassidy would send one of her officers over to Alistair's house to make sure Eva wasn't there. I had no idea where else she could be. I also assumed that Cassidy had sent somebody to talk to the pirate crew to see if they knew anything.

But, like I said, I was not involved with this. Even if I wanted to be. I was going to keep myself as focused as a cameraman waiting for the perfect shot.

Rick cleared his throat as we all stood around stupefied after Alistair's arrest. "We all need to call it a day. Let's meet again in the morning, and we'll see if there are any updates. Until then, I think we could all use a break."

No one argued, but most of us were quiet as we walked away.

I headed to my trailer, changed, and grabbed my phone before stepping back outside to meet Jackson.

He took my hand as we headed toward his truck and climbed inside.

"What a day," Jackson muttered. "What are you thinking?"

I shivered in spite of myself. "I just can't believe Alistair would stoop that low. Do you think he's a killer?"

"If somebody is willing to do all those things out of jealousy, then there's no telling what else he might do."

"I'm not Alistair's biggest fan, but I have a hard time believing he'd kill somebody."

"You and I have been involved with enough murders and investigations together to know that it's not always the person who *seems* like the killer who *is* the killer."

"You're right," I said. "I just don't like any of this. I should've said no to this film, and I should've just gone to Nags Head and tried to live a normal life for this two-week break. But, instead, I had to say yes to this movie and land in the middle of another murder."

Jackson squeezed my hand. "You were trying to do it as a favor to Alistair. It was a kind gesture. It just didn't turn out that well."

"Thank you for always seeing the best in me. That means a lot."

Jackson reached for my face, and his hand gently brushed my cheek and jaw as he gazed at me. "I always want to believe the best in you, Joey."

My hands covered his. "What did I do to deserve you?"

"I ask myself all the time what I did to deserve you."

"Then I guess we're both in a good place if we're wondering what we did to deserve each other."

We shared a smile.

"I guess we should get back to the house now," I said. "We still have a whole crew there waiting for us. Hopefully, they were able to have some fun on the island today without us. I still feel a little guilty that I'm not able to spend more time with them."

"They knew when they came that you were going to be busy. They just wanted to be with you when they could."

"That means a lot to me." But even as I said the words my mind was still on this investigation. I wanted to know what was going on here. I wanted answers.

As I sat back and we started down the road, my mind drifted toward the list of numbers that had been in Bucky's pocket when his body was discovered. What did they mean?

I had already gone through the most obvious

choices. I didn't believe the numbers were a locker combination or any type of coordinates. But if that's not what they were, then what did those numbers mean? There had to be a reason Bucky had them in his pocket with my name on them.

My thoughts turned the numbers over again and again. Maybe we would figure it out sometime. We just needed more time.

At that moment, my phone buzzed. I'd gotten a text.

I gaped at what I saw there.

It was a picture of Eva.

Someone had cut her hair off.

Below the photo were the words, "Beauty is only skin deep."

I grabbed my phone. I had to call Cassidy. Now.

CHAPTER
TWENTY-SEVEN

THE FIRST THING I did the next morning was to check my email.

I felt the blood drain from my face when I saw a new email from "Alistair." With Jackson sitting beside me at the kitchen table, I clicked on it.

As suspected, it was a revised script.

"What's different?" Jackson asked.

I scrolled through the pages until I finally came to a stop at the end. I swallowed hard when I realized the alterations. "In this version, everyone in the movie dies at the end during an explosion."

"Do you think . . ." I couldn't finish the question.

"I wouldn't put it past the killer to go to extreme measures like this."

"Me neither. But if Alistair is in jail, who sent this?

Maybe he's telling the truth and he didn't alter the script."

"You can schedule emails to go out. He could have planned this before he was arrested."

That might be correct, but, for some reason, I couldn't see it.

I glanced at Jackson, a new plan forming in my mind. "I have an idea."

"What's that?"

"I think we should try to continue filming today —with or without Alistair. Because this killer is obviously getting desperate. He's going to strike again. And what better way to catch him than by luring him out."

Jackson did his whole jaw-flexing thing before shaking his head. "I'm not sure that's such a good idea."

"What do we have to lose?"

Jackson leveled his gaze with me. "Everything. We have everything to lose."

I opened my mouth, wanting to argue. But I couldn't. Because Jackson was right. If this plan didn't work, then someone else could die.

We had a lot to think through.

But if we arranged it just right, then maybe it would provide us with some answers.

First, I'd have to talk to Cassidy about it.

Jackson was talking to Cassidy on the phone as we arrived on the set. I was the last one to get there, it appeared.

As I watched the cast and crew a moment, I couldn't help but note that everyone seemed to be moving like zombies. Everyone was dazed. Who could blame them in a situation like this?

As I continued to scan everyone, I pictured imaginary closeups of each person with background commentary running, as if this situation were a movie instead of real life.

As the thought entered my mind, I sucked in a breath.

"What is it?" Jackson put his phone away and turned to me.

How could I not have seen this before?

"Jackson . . . tell me if I'm crazy but . . . I think everyone here has been targeted in their own way."

A knot formed between his brows. "What do you mean?"

"Think about it—about everyone's weakness. Alistair, his weakness is always wanting to be in control, so someone targeted that by taking control away for this movie. Someone knew that changing the script would drive Alistair mad."

"Keep going."

"Washington. Someone left a six pack outside his door, tempting him to start drinking again in the middle of this tumultuous, stress-inducing situation."

"Still listening." His eyes sparked, as if he thought my theory might be valid.

"Eva? Vanity. That's why they cut her hair. Sarah? Money. She has student loans to pay and her livelihood is being threatened right now. Rick? Perfection. Everything about this film is going wrong. Mindy? Making things beautiful. The tips of her makeup brushes were cut."

"And you?"

I swallowed hard. "Danger. I've been one of the only ones getting direct threats to my physical well-being."

"What about Sai and Brandon?"

I shook my head. "I'm not sure. I don't know them well enough yet. But am I going crazy or does that make sense?"

Jackson's jaw flexed again. "I think you might be onto something, Joey. This whole cast and crew have been a target. But why?"

I shook my head. "That's a great question. Maybe today will hold some answers."

His gaze darkened like he was still uncomfortable

with this whole plan. "I talked to Cassidy. She and her team are going to come and provide some extra security here."

"Great. What about Alistair? Eva? Any updates?"

He shook his head. "No, not yet."

CHAPTER TWENTY-EIGHT

I TOLD Rick my thoughts on picking up with the production, and he agreed.

"I know enough about the film and the direction Alistair wants to go that I think I can act as a temporary director until Alistair is released. I've worked with him enough to have a good feel for the way he does things."

I stared at him a moment, hardly hearing anything beyond his statement about Alistair's future.

"Until Alistair is released?" I repeated. "You don't think he's guilty, do you?"

He shrugged. "Why would he do this? It doesn't make any sense."

"Does it really make sense for anyone to do this?"

"Point taken. I don't know. Maybe Alistair is

guilty. Sometimes he does seem like he has a screw loose. Either way, I think we should do what we have to do today. You don't have much time left, and there are some storms out to sea that could come up this way next week. The more we can get done, the better."

"I'll go get suited up then." A surge of satisfaction welled in me. Maybe today would be the day we actually got some answers.

Though I had some reservations about the movie itself, I had to remember that there were other people whose careers were on the line here besides mine. There were people like Sarah who needed this project so they could have a paycheck. Did I want to be the bratty person who dropped out just because I was feeling a little miserable?

Besides, the net was getting smaller. Washington wasn't guilty. Alistair was behind bars, and Eva was still missing.

Who did that leave?

There was Larry, the security guard. I supposed if I wanted to broaden my suspects, I could include the rest of the cast and crew who hadn't been eliminated. That would be Mindy, Sarah, Rick, Brandon, and Sai.

Being on set today might be the perfect way to weed some people out.

I went over to the makeup trailer and found

Mindy inside. Not only was she inside, but she looked upset. I could tell by the red around her eyes that she'd been crying.

I sat down across from her. "What's going on?"

"Oh, Joey. I couldn't sleep all night. I kept thinking about what had happened."

"I know. We're all upset over what's going on."

"No, you don't understand," she said with a sniffle. "Alistair didn't do this."

I stared at her, uncertain if I had heard her correctly. After a moment of silence, I said, "What do you mean? He admitted he paid Bucky to do this."

"I know," she said. "But the night when that man died? Alistair didn't do it."

"How could you possibly know that?"

"Because I was with him."

"Wait." I stared at Mindy. "You and Alistair?"

That was her sweater I'd found in Alistair's bathroom. Suddenly, it all made sense.

"Yes, it's true." Mindy glanced down at her hands, tears welling her eyes. "I knew we were nothing serious, that I was just another one of his girls. He's always dating people who mean absolutely nothing to him. But I've had a mad crush on him ever since I saw his first movie."

"Wait, you honestly like Alistair?" I couldn't even imagine what that would be like. There was nothing about this new Alistair that I admired in any way, shape, or form. In a world where people could be anything, no one should be King. Alistair King, that was.

She nodded. "It's crazy, I know. It doesn't make any sense. Why would I like someone who was that self-centered? But I've always fallen for the wrong guy."

"Aren't you the one who told me about him and Eva?"

She nodded, guilt filling her gaze. "I know. I was just trying to take any attention off of me. I didn't want anyone to know. I didn't want to be one of those girls."

"Oh Mindy," I muttered.

I really didn't know what else to say. I liked Mindy. I liked her a lot. I would've never guessed she'd put herself in a situation like this.

Finally, I asked, "Why didn't you tell the police this?"

"Because I knew how it would look. I knew that once word got out, everybody would know and judge me. I should've said something. I knew I should have. But I was just so nervous about it."

"You're going to have to go down to the police station and share this information," I said. "You know that, right?"

Mindy nodded, her eyes still tear-filled.

There was one other thing that bugged me. If Alistair wasn't guilty, that meant the real killer was still out there.

It also made Mindy the most likely suspect in Eva's disappearance because she had the best motive: jealousy.

AS I STEPPED out of the trailer, I saw Jackson waiting outside. Based on his expression, he was trying to figure out something.

"What's going on?" I asked, joining him on the sandy ground.

He held his phone, displaying a snapshot of the message that had been found in Bucky's pocket. "I've been studying these numbers."

"Do you have a lead?"

"Maybe. I have a thought, at least. Could I see the original script?"

"Sure." I hurried back into my trailer, found it, and handed it to Jackson. "What now?"

"I know this is going to sound crazy, but there was an episode of *Relentless* where someone left Raven Remington a secret message. But, in order to figure out what it was, she had to match the line number, page number, and a word number from a technology manual. What if somebody did the same thing, except using the original script?"

My eyebrows shot in the air. "I think it's worth a shot."

Jackson rattled off the first three numbers. I went to the seventeenth page, I found the fifth line of text, and the twelfth word.

"Joey," I told Jackson. "That's the twelfth word."

He wrote it down on a pad of paper he always kept in his pocket. "Okay, let's keep going and see what we can figure out."

Jackson read the next line of numbers.

I found them after a couple minutes and said, "someone."

We went through this for several more minutes until we had the words, "Joey, someone is trying to kill you."

Not exactly what I wanted to hear.

But there was more.

We still had about thirty more words to look up. Somebody was definitely trying to send me a coded message. I had no idea why he would go through all of this trouble instead of just simply writing the words. But at least we were getting somewhere.

"I'm going to try to figure this out while you're

filming," Jackson said. "Cassidy has her men here also. There's a gun in the final scene. I checked it, just to make sure, and it is a fake."

I squeezed his arm. "Thank you."

Because the last thing I wanted was to go out with a bang.

"You're on their side?" I said to Washington George as we both stood on the beach staring at each other. "I knew I couldn't trust you."

A storm lingered in the distance, making this the perfect time to shoot my final scene. Alistair couldn't have asked for better or more atmospheric conditions if he'd tried.

Washington stared back at me, his face transformed into that of someone sinister. Gone was the young CIA recruit who'd been sent to find Drusilla Fairweather and obtain confidential information from her. The double agent in him had emerged, and he was desperate.

"Everyone at the CIA thought that you were the crème de la crème," he muttered. "But you're not, and you never were. People are going to look back at your life and say Drusilla who? It's going to be like you never existed and you never mattered."

Hearing Washington say those words reminded me of the bitterness Alistair must've felt as he wrote the script. Because these lines weren't just about Drusilla in the story, were they?

No, they were about his true feelings toward me. He wanted to make sure that one day I didn't matter either. Bitterness sure could mess a person up. That was why I'd vowed to try to get rid of the bitterness in my own life.

I continued to stare at Washington as he faced me on the beach. The wind whipped around us. He drew a gun and pointed it at me.

"Let's just get this over with," he said. "There's no need to extend this, and we both know what's going to happen."

"You're going to kill me," I said. "That's what all of this has been about, hasn't it?"

"I am sorry that it has to end this way," Washington said. "But you've left me with no choice."

"There's always a choice. You don't have to do this."

"Yes, I do. You don't even understand. You've lived your life as the golden spy girl for so long. You could've reveled in it. Instead you came to this desolate island to be by yourself. But, even then, people still didn't forget you. I need to ensure that your life is erased."

"Don't you know that if a person dies before their time, they always become an instant hero?"

Washington stared at me. "That's not true."

I listed people to prove it was.

"Okay, enough talking!" he shouted. "It's time for this to end."

He extended the gun toward me.

Just then, my phone buzzed. I'd kept it in my pocket.

I had a choice to make. Check to see who this text message was from.

Or wait until we finished filming.

However, even with that fake gun pointed at me, I couldn't help but think this could be something important.

After all, this wasn't done yet.

As the camera panned to Washington, I glanced in my pocket. Jackson had finished decoding the message.

> Joey, someone is trying to kill you in real life. Be careful. X marks the spot —of a killer. I saw him messing with the script and your picture was on the screen.

X marks the spot of a killer? What did that even mean?

And why had Bucky written in code?

I only had one possible explanation.

Maybe he'd done it for the same reason he'd pretended to want to hire me and Jackson. He wanted to get a firsthand look into my life.

For that matter, what if he'd written in code to put an interesting spin on the article? What if he wanted to watch me figure all of it out? It would be an inside look into my life and into how I'd managed to solve several mysteries in the past.

Maybe he didn't even really think I'd die. Maybe he'd just said that to act as an inciting incident. Just like he'd most likely made up that threat and written it out to himself.

"Joey?" Rick asked.

My gaze came back into focus, and I remembered what I was doing here.

"It's your line," Rick reminded us. "Let's take it from 'It's time for this to end.' Action."

Washington stared at me again and repeated the line.

As I stared at the gun, a terrible thought went through my head.

X marks the spot of a killer.

Bucky had figured out who the killer was, hadn't he? Maybe he wanted to warn me. I didn't know for sure.

I stared at the barrel.

That looked like a fake gun. I knew Jackson even said he'd checked it.

But I remembered all those altered scripts.

I remembered everything that had happened.

What if somebody had managed to substitute a real gun after all?

Panic raced through me.

X marks the spot.

He wasn't talking about a treasure map, was he?

I sucked in a breath. I knew who was behind this.

And this person would have had the chance to substitute the fake gun for a real one—even after Jackson had inspected it.

CHAPTER
THIRTY

"WAIT!" I shouted. "Don't do it!"

I saw the flash of confusion in Washington's eyes. Did my costar still think I was acting? That's how it appeared.

"Here's the thing." His finger remained on the trigger, and his voice made it clear he was still in character. "No more talking. I'm sorry that it has to end this way."

"Don't do it!" I shouted. "It's a real gun!"

The confused look returned to his eyes. Washington had no idea what I was doing, did he?

He thrust his Glock forward. "Of course, I have a real gun. How else would I kill you except with a real gun?"

I braced myself. I knew what was coming.

Washington was going to pull that trigger. But,

instead of a fake bullet coming out, it would be a real bullet. And it was going to pierce me. Maybe even kill me.

I looked around, but there was nowhere for me to hide.

This was it.

I was going to die right here.

As everyone turned at a commotion in the distance, Jackson flew from the crowd.

He tackled Washington to the ground. The two wrestled until Jackson grabbed the gun and backed away.

"Someone switched the fake gun for a real one," Jackson said. "This was after I checked the weapon earlier today."

"But I had my eyes on that guy all day," Sarah said. "Just like you told me."

"Not all day." Jackson raised the gun in the air and pulled the trigger. A loud bang filled the air.

Everyone on set froze. There was now no doubt the gun was real.

"I . . ." Sarah wrung her hands together. "I did leave it for just a minute to run to the bathroom. I guess it could have been switched out then. I'm so sorry. I had no idea."

"You can't blame me this time."

My head jerked toward the voice. It was Alistair.

He was back, a haggard look in his eyes, his poof flat, and his clothes wrinkled.

"I'll have you all know I was cleared." He scowled. "So now I'm back, and you're all under contract, and we need to wrap up this film."

"Not until we figure out what's going on here." Jackson turned to address everyone. "Someone who is here on this set right now replaced the fake gun with a real gun. Someone is trying to kill my fiancée, and no one is leaving here until we know who is behind this."

"He's correct." Cassidy stepped from the woods, and her officers also appeared, scooting closer.

"I know who did it," I said. Finally, it was my Scooby Doo moment.

"Who do you think did this, Joey?" Jackson asked, his voice tense enough for a high-wire act.

My gaze met that of everyone around me. With lightning and thunder in the background, I began to spell out my theory.

"Originally, we thought it was Alistair."

As I said the words, I pulled off my wig, realizing I looked entirely too ridiculous to be taken seriously dressed like this. I tossed it onto the sand and continued to peel off the layers from my face along with my false teeth.

"And Alistair, on one hand, has a great motive—

to make me look bad," I continued. "But, on the other hand, he has a very bad motive because in making me look bad, he would also make himself look bad. Plus, he has an alibi on the night Bucky was killed."

Murmurs went around the group.

"I also wondered if Mindy might be behind it, but Alistair and Mindy both have an alibi. However, Mindy had a motive to dislike Eva. We still don't know where Eva is. But, like I said, Mindy has an alibi so she can't be guilty either."

More chatter sounded.

I continued, feeling like an imaginary spotlight was shining on me at center stage. "I considered that it may have been Washington. But he also has an alibi for the night Bucky died. We're slowly whittling down who could be guilty."

"Why does it have to be someone who's here on this set?" Rick asked. "Why can't it be one of those pirates?"

"Because, as pirates, they didn't have access to the script," I said.

"Why is this killer changing the script so much?" Mindy asked. "It doesn't make any sense. Why would someone toy with us like this?"

"Because the script has been the target here, along with Alistair. The bad guy is someone who has a lot of bitter feelings toward Alistair."

Everyone turned to look at Alistair as soon as his name left my lips.

"Why would someone want to ruin me?" Alistair pointed to himself, pure shock on his face.

"Because of the way you treat people," I stated.

"But what about Bucky?" Sarah asked.

"Alistair gave Bucky a copy of the script," I said. "Maybe it was part of the negotiation process for the photos."

Based on Alistair's scowl, I would assume that was true.

"But Bucky wasn't the one who altered it. I'll get back to that." I scanned everyone. "I need to finish spelling out Bucky's role in this first. Bucky just happened to be in the wrong place at the wrong time. He came to meet with the Piranha, also known as Alistair—though Bucky probably didn't know that at the time."

I glanced at Alistair again. He didn't deny any of this.

"As Bucky walked onto the set, he looked for the Piranha, but stumbled across the killer instead. He realized what was happening, that someone was messing with the script."

No one said anything. They all waited for me to continue.

So I did. "The killer saw Bucky and knew he'd

been caught. He also knew that if word leaked about what he'd done, he'd never get away with his scheme. Knowing what I do about Bucky, he may have even snapped some pictures of this person to use as blackmail. The bad guy felt like he had no choice but to kill Bucky."

A gasp went around the circle.

"Who would want to threaten all of us?" Washington asked. "I still don't understand. All we're trying to do is make a living here."

"And therein lies the problem." My gaze scanned the circle and stopped at one person. "I'm looking at the killer right now."

CHAPTER
THIRTY-ONE

ANOTHER GASP SOUNDED.

Rick pointed the finger at himself. "Why would I be behind this?"

"A few reasons," I said. "But mostly because X marks the spot."

"What does that mean?" Rick's voice rose with confusion.

I had a feeling everyone else was as puzzled as Rick about my statement.

I raised a hand as I talked out my theory. I pictured it all playing out in my head. "Bucky was out here taking pictures. He actually photographed you messing with the script. He also saw my picture on your computer screen, and he knew you were up to something. Maybe he didn't quite know what or the extent of it, but he knew it was trouble. Whenever he could, I'm going to guess, he was hanging out in the woods near the set, eavesdropping on everything he could."

"If that was true, why would this guy send you a coded message?" Rick asked. "If he feared for your life, he should have told you instead of playing games."

"I did a little research and discovered that Bucky was unconventional. He liked to get creative for his stories, and he wasn't above being deceitful. He wrote that message in code, and he wanted to be on hand to see if I figured it out. I don't think he actually thought I was going to die. He only knew something wasn't right, and he wanted to stir up trouble. Since he was sneaking onto the set that evening anyway, he'd planned on leaving it at my trailer."

"Sounds like a stretch," Rick muttered.

"What it boils down to is the fact that Bucky saw all of this as an opportunity both to get to know me better and to add some *ump* to his article. It was like he lived in an alternate world—much like when he pretended to be a pirate. This was a game to him. He decided to tell me that you were up to something by telling me that X marks the culprit."

"You're saying I have an X on me?" Rick asked.

I nodded. "On your cheek. That scar. It looks like an X. In fact, it must have shown up in some of

Bucky's photos. That's why you destroyed his camera. You probably threw it out into the ocean, if I had to guess."

Rick didn't say anything for a couple of seconds until, "Why would I go through all this trouble?"

"I was hoping you'd ask that," I said. "Easy. Because Alistair has promised you your big break for years. Yet he's never given it to you. You've given him a script that you felt had potential. He promised you the world. Yet he's still only kept you as a lowly cameraman."

Rick scoffed.

"You wrote *A Pirate's Life*, didn't you? You wanted Alistair to take that on as his next project. He probably even promised you he would."

Rick said nothing, which I took as a sign I was correct.

"You've had years and years for this bitterness to develop," I started. "You wanted to mess with Alistair's head. At first . . . But when Bucky got in the way, things took a turn for the worse, and you knew you had to take care of things."

"You don't have any proof." Rick narrowed his eyes. "This is all conjecture."

"Maybe it is, but you know I'm telling the truth," I said. "You're the one who is behind this. Now, where is Eva? What did she have to do with this?"

"I have no idea."

Cassidy stepped forward. "Rick, I think we should go down to the station to talk."

"I think we're doing fine right here." Rick's voice sounded below a growl.

As she reached for his arm, he quickly withdrew something from his waistband.

A gun.

He raised it toward all of us, and his eyes bulged as he said, "Everyone, stand down. This isn't the way this was supposed to end."

Everyone seemed to freeze as we anticipated what would happen next.

This couldn't end well.

Rick had one gun pointed, at times, at all of us.

But Jackson, Cassidy, and two of her officers had guns pointed at Rick.

Even if Rick shot one of us, there was no way he was walking out of this alive. He had to know that.

"Why'd you do this, Rick?" Cassidy asked. "Why'd you resort to murder?"

His hand shook. "Joey was right. Everyone keeps offering me empty promises, but nothing has come from them. I've been working in this industry for twenty years, and this whole time I've been waiting for my big break. It's never come."

"So you blame everyone else?" Cassidy asked.

As she spoke, I scooted backward, away from Rick. Washington saw me and slowly began to scoot back also.

"It's hard to see everyone around you prospering while you suffer."

"Why are you suffering, Rick?" Cassidy continued.

I backed up another step until I reached Jackson. He nudged me behind him.

"I've never gotten my big break," he said. "I haven't even met the woman of my dreams yet. My whole life has been consumed by this industry, yet it's done nothing for me except take from me."

"You could have gotten out," I said. "Or tried to do your own film, to make your own way."

"You don't think I thought of that! I did. I did try. It never worked out. Do you even realize how much work I put into this? I try to make things perfect. Yet my life is a mess."

"You didn't have to kill Bucky," Jackson said.

"He realized what I was up to and tried to blackmail me. We met in the lighthouse, and . . . I never meant for things to go this far."

"Are you sure you didn't mean for them to go

further?" Jackson asked. "As in, blowing up this set while everyone was working?"

Murmurs sounded around us.

"It just started with the script." Ricks' nostril's flared. "I wanted to mess with Alistair. But then, once I got on set, everyone started driving me crazy."

"So you decided to play on everyone's weakness," I finished.

His eyes lit with surprise. "Exactly. How did you know?"

I shrugged. "I figured it out. You even made it seem like someone was toying with you, causing your OCD to act up."

"Did you send those pirates here also?" Jackson asked.

He smirked, but it quickly disappeared. "I gave the pirates that treasure map, knowing they'd wander onto the set and mess things up. It was just one more way of putting Alistair in his place. It seemed innocent."

Things were falling in place but . . . "The one thing I don't understand is why things escalated."

"No one was supposed to die. It just happened. And then I realized I was probably going to jail anyway. I decided, why not go out with a bang." Rick held the gun away from himself, flopping his arm to the side and leaving his chest wide open as if inviting death. "Why don't you just shoot me now?"

"We don't want to do that." Cassidy took a step closer, her voice even and calm as she approached him. "We want to talk this through."

"There's no talking necessary here. It's already been done."

"Where's Eva?" Cassidy asked.

"She's at Alistair's," Rick said. "I left her there this morning. I have a camera recording her every move. She's going crazy. I cut her hair." He smirked.

I let out a quick breath. He really was awful. And twisted. And so messed up.

"Put the gun down, Rick," Cassidy said.

I expected him to fight back. To argue.

Instead, he lowered it to the sand.

As he did, Cassidy's officers rushed toward him and slapped handcuffs on his wrists.

Maybe this was finally over.

Unlike the movie—which had a twist at the end revealing to the audience it had all been a virtual reality game—this was all real. Too real.

But at least no one else had gotten hurt.

CHAPTER
THIRTY-TWO

TWO HOURS LATER, the cast and crew were packing up.

This film would be no more.

Even though I hated the fact that I'd wasted my time with this movie, another part of me was glad it was over and my name would no longer be attached.

Saying yes to this project had been a mistake. Mostly because saying yes to *A Useless Ending to a Hard-Fought Life* had been saying no to Jackson and our *Happy-Ever-After Ending to a Hard-Sought Love*.

The irony of the name Alistair had given to this film wasn't lost on me. He'd wanted me to feel useless, hadn't he? Professional jealousy had led him down a treacherous path.

The same for Rick. The desire to get ahead had

clouded his judgment and eventually had overtaken him.

If we weren't careful, dark emotions could ruin us. I'd be wise to keep that in mind also. The moment we thought we were above it was the moment pride stepped in and showed us our true colors.

I'd also realized with absolute clarity that I didn't want my life to be useless. I didn't want my fame to be for my benefit or at the expense of the people I loved. Because I knew myself, I knew it would be something I had to constantly remind myself of.

As Jackson and I stood on the shore, in the shadow of the lighthouse, I closed my eyes a minute and reviewed everything that had just gone down.

Each person here on set had been questioned.

Rick had been arrested.

Eva had been located at Alistair's, just as Rick said, and she was now at a local clinic being checked out. Initial reports were that she was shaken but fine.

My gaze drifted toward a figure trudging across the sand toward Jackson and me. Cassidy. She'd had her work cut out for her this week.

"Good job, you two," she said, pausing in front of us. "Thanks for all your help."

"No problem," Jackson said. "I'm just glad we could help before anyone else got hurt."

"And if you ever want to leave Nags Head and

look for a new job, things are pretty exciting here on our little island." She flashed a smile.

Jackson nodded, raising an eyebrow. "I've noticed."

Cassidy turned to me. "And Joey . . . it was so nice to meet you. I can't wait to find out what happens with Raven Remington."

"I think you'll like this new season that's coming up."

"I'm sure I will. I wish the two of you the best of luck together. Come back to visit our little island when you have the chance."

"We will," I said.

With a wave, Cassidy nodded and walked away.

I turned to Jackson as we stood there on the beach, the ocean waves crashing behind us. The storm still remained offshore, giving us a fabulous show and reminding us of the danger we'd narrowly missed.

"I guess we have some time together after all." Jackson's hands went to my waist, and he pulled me closer.

"I guess we do." I let out a breath as a thought hit me. It might be crazy but . . . "We could get married now, you know."

His eyebrows shot up. "Right now? As in, today?"

I shrugged, realizing I hadn't thought any of this through. But maybe this was the solution we'd been looking for. "Yes, today. I mean, we're here. We have time. Why not?"

He rubbed my arms and took a step back. Something about his reaction caused me to brace myself for whatever he had to say. I sensed a shift in our conversation—a shift that might not be what I wanted.

"Part of me wants to say yes," Jackson started. "I'd love nothing more than to call you my wife. But . . ."

I held my breath, fearing he'd changed his mind. Or that he needed space. Or that he'd seen the cracks in our relationship, the cracks in me. I'd programmed myself to think that all good things needed to come to an end. And since Jackson seemed too good to be true . . .

His gaze bore into mine, his eyes orbs of hazel and green that mesmerized me every time. "But Joey. . . when we get married, I don't want it to be because we had an opening in our schedules. I want it to be purposeful and planned. I want it to be . . . I don't know. Special, I suppose."

His words rolled over me. "I understand."

He rubbed my arms, and his voice softened.

"That is not a rejection. It's anything but. You deserve a wedding that screams, 'Joey.'"

"Red carpet, flying bullets, stalkers—"

He chuckled. "No, all the other parts of you. It should be beautiful and fun and full of love. Full of the people who are important to us." His smile slipped. "I don't want to start our marriage flippantly, giving it just as little thought as we'd give going to a movie or out to eat. You're too important to me."

Tears rushed to my eyes. "You're important to me also. I'm sorry if I haven't shown that."

"You have, Joey."

I tried to hold the moisture back, but it escaped from my eyes anyway. "Listen, we have next week together. Let's nail down the date and reserve what we need to reserve. How does that sound?"

A grin spread across his face. "That sounds fantastic."

My heart felt like it could melt into a puddle. "I love you, Jackson Sullivan."

"I love you too, Joey. And, the truth is, life will never be normal and boring with you around. And I wouldn't have it any other way."

As he said the words, I reached up to kiss him. A sound in the distance stopped me before I could.

A vehicle pulled up on scene.

I grinned as I recognized it.

The Hot Chicks, Phoebe, and Zane had arrived.

They must have heard what happened and come to check on us.

As they surrounded us, cackling about cotton ball diets, how one of the Hot Chicks was crushing on the Lantern Beach mayor, and verbally hashtagging things like #lifeisneverboringwithJoey, I smiled. I was thankful for this crazy community around me—each and every person.

But most of all for Jackson.

~~~

Thank you so much for reading *Joke and Dagger*. If you enjoyed this book, please consider leaving a review!

Keep reading for a preview of *Wreck the Halls*.

NOW AVAILABLE

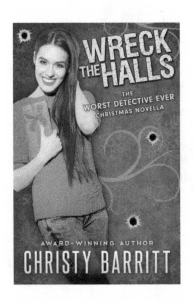

WRECK THE HALLS:
CHAPTER ONE

"What's this show you're guest hosting called again?" Jackson Sullivan crossed his arms and leaned against his police SUV. It was parked in the driveway outside a rental home as we waited for a caravan of vehicles to meet us.

I pulled my winter white coat closer as a frigid wind came over the ocean and spread its icy fingers over the sandy landscape—and over me. "It's called *Lit.*"

He squinted, looking unaffected by the cold— unlike me as I danced and jumped around to stay warm. "Doesn't that mean drunk?"

"It *used* to mean drunk. Now, in the current vernacular, it means excited or hyped." I positioned my hands into peace signs, mimicking every Instagrammer out there, and even added duck lips. "You know, as in, that party was *lit*."

Jackson grunted as if he still didn't believe me. Or like he thought I'd lost it. Maybe both.

"Anyway, *Lit* is a TV special that will feature some of the best decorated homes in the country at Christmastime," I said. "The families chosen to have their houses featured will also have money donated to a charity on their behalf."

"Sounds noble."

"It is. And fun. And festive. And all that's merry and bright!"

"Kind of like you."

"You're so sweet that I could marry you." I stepped closer and grabbed the scarf around Jackson's neck. I'd given the red cashmere piece to him myself and thought it looked nice with his black leather jacket. I tugged him closer to me. "It's going to be a great show."

A smile started at the corner of Jackson's lips. "Is it?"

"Yes. You're going to love it." I continued pulling him closer until I was able to plant a kiss on his lips. "I'm so glad my friend talked me into hosting it with her."

Only five more months and I would be able to call this man my husband. I couldn't wait. We still had so much wedding planning to do, though. At least we'd been having fun picking everything out lately. We'd tasted cakes, sampled menus, checked out potential honeymoon spots. It was the perfect way to spend my time off work.

"At least I'll get to have you here and all to myself for the next month," Jackson murmured, wrapping his arms around my waist.

"Exactly. Except for this week. This week, we'll film *Lit*. I have a couple of press opportunities, a charity dinner, and the Christmas parade."

"Is that all?" He raised his eyebrows, his words dryly sarcastic.

I shrugged. "That's it. And you get to act as my personal security. Thank you, Mayor Allen."

"Whatever I can do to serve my city."

I was about to flirt some more when three SUVs pulled into the driveway. The crew had arrived. I stepped away from Jackson, trying not to be one of those PDA couples, but I instantly missed his warmth.

Now that the crew had arrived, we only had an hour to debrief and go over all the details before we headed over to the filming site. Our schedule would be tight, but this was going to be fun.

Especially because . . .

"Starla!" I let out a squeal as my friend's head

appeared out of the back door of the black Expedition.

It had been so long since I'd seen my best friend. So. Long. And I missed her like Scooby would miss Shaggy, or Thelma would miss Louise. I mean, not enough to drive my car off a cliff but . . . you get the drift.

She hopped out and ran toward me, a matching squeal escaping from her. "Joey Darling! I can't believe we're finally seeing each other!"

"It's been too long."

We hugged, kissed each other's cheeks, and squealed some more. We were totally cliché BFFs, and I didn't even care.

I stepped back, still squeezing her arms, and studied my friend. She looked different since I'd last seen her. "Your hair!"

She was known for her long, luxurious blonde locks. But her new do was short, honey blonde, and almost boyish.

"It's for a new role in the *Gladiator Diaries*," she said. "Did I tell you I got the lead role in that one?"

I twisted my head. This was the first I'd heard of it. "The movie with Dwayne 'The Rock' Johnson? No, I had no idea."

"Totally. It's like the *Gladiator* meets *The Princess*

Diaries. My agent thinks it will be a smashing success."

"Sounds like quite the combination." How could it not be?

Memories of my last movie floated back to me. It had been like James Bond meets *Driving Miss Daisy*, and I still thanked God every day it had fallen through. But that was just me.

"It is. Anyway, the director asked me to cut my hair for the role." She reached for the nape of her neck and rubbed her hand there, looking uncertain. "I didn't want to do something this extreme, but I did it anyway. I decided to take one for the team."

"It's cute." Starla would look good if she shaved her head bald. She was that type of person—tiny and perky with delicate features. Sometimes she could be a bit of an airhead, but it was in an endearing way. Besides, she was a ton of fun to be around.

"Thanks, girlfriend." She looped her arm through mine. "Now, are you ready to do this Christmas special?"

"Ready as Rudolph on Christmas Eve."

As the rest of the crew scrambled around us to move their things inside, Starla's gaze drifted over my shoulder, and her smile brightened. "You must be the Hubba Hubba Hunka Hunka Jackson."

"Oh, I'm so sorry." I shrugged with overly dramatic guilt and maybe even a little embarrassment over her word choice. "I forgot to introduce you!"

Jackson stepped toward her and extended his hand. "Nice to meet you."

"Oh, it's even nicer to meet you," Starla gushed. "I've heard so much about you. All good. Apparently, you put every hero on every TV show to shame."

"I don't know if I'd say *that*." He shrugged, always humble when he had every reason to be cocky. Maybe not *always* humble and *never* cocky, but close enough.

"I *would* say that. Joey would *never* exaggerate." Starla grinned, looking as charming as always as she elbowed me. "I have no reason to doubt her."

I took Starla's arm before she embarrassed Jackson anymore. We needed a subject change. "Are you ready for this?"

"Are you kidding? This is going to make our star power rise. You know what that means? Cha-ching!"

I smiled while inwardly cringing. She reminded me so much of my old life. The life I'd tried to leave behind. For the most part, I had for almost the past year.

But I didn't want to be the kind of person who sought after tabloid exposure or who acted crazy just for more press time. I hoped my time around Starla wouldn't push me back into my old ways.

No, it wouldn't. I was stronger than that. Life and experience had changed me.

I decided to change the subject. "So, is Thompson here?"

Thompson Aims was the producer of this show. *Lit* had been filmed in seven different locations so far, and different celebrities had hosted each place. Now, it was our turn here in Nags Head, North Carolina. Starla and I were the last to film.

Christmas was only four weeks away, so our episode would air right before Christmas day. The show would not only highlight families and towns, but also charities and small-town traditions. All in all, it was a win-win-win!

"I think I saw Thompson scurry past," Starla said. "I know he wants to explain to us how everything will go down this week."

"Makes sense."

"Have I ever told you just how much I *love* Christmas? This whole experience is going to be the *bomb*."

The bomb . . . lit . . . I was seeing a theme here.

Explosions.

I only hoped that the explosion was of the good variety . . . an explosion of love and giving and peace on earth.

Because in my experience, explosions meant danger and crime and being chased by bad guys.

Over the next hour, Thompson debriefed Starla and me on how everything would go down today. What the process would be. How much time we had.

Jackson had also met with Thompson to run through how things would go tonight. They'd expected big crowds, which meant a police presence was needed.

After that, Starla and I went to hair and makeup. As much as I loved the end result of hair and makeup, I hated the process. Looking good wasn't easy.

But finally, I was done. Thankfully, the show had provided us everything we needed, as Starla's luggage had apparently gotten lost at the airport.

I'd been clothed in black leggings with a white tunic top, an adorable black leather jacket, and a green and red plaid scarf. Starla had been assigned a coordinating outfit of white leggings, a green tunic, and a maroon-colored duster sweater.

Finally, we were set.

Jackson would come with us as part of a security detail. You know, just in case. Because in my world, just in cases happened all the time. So Jackson had insisted on being present . . . wait for it . . . *just in case*.

The mayor of Nags Head was on board for all of this because he wanted as much positive press for the area as he could possibly get, especially now that he was running for senator. The election was still a year away, but he was in full campaign mode.

That led Starla and I up to this moment: the moment when we were ready for show time.

Our caravan of SUVs pulled into a little neighborhood on the west side of the island. This was the area where full-timers were more likely to live—away from the ocean and the homes close to the shore where tourists flocked.

All kinds of different homes graced the hilly streets—traditionally stilted beach homes, brick ranches, and even some colonials. It was eclectic, but I liked eclectic. Several homes were decorated modestly for the upcoming holiday.

Before we even reached our destination, I could see the crowds had started to gather in the street.

This was going to be interesting.

It was only three in the afternoon. The real show wouldn't start until the sun went down at five or so. I felt confident everything would go according to plan, especially since Thompson Aims was at the helm.

The man was legendary for TV specials like this.

They were each heartwarming, fun, and feel-good. The man himself was on the quieter side. He had an affection for fedoras, which matched his chunky glasses and soft voice.

"So, you meet the family," Thompson said as we approached the house in the Expedition. "You hear their story. Then you tour their home and *ooh* and *ahh* over all their decorations. This is a kind show. No mean comments."

I was kind of appalled he even had to say that. As far as I knew, I didn't have a reputation of being a jerk . . . did I? "Of course."

He offered a brief shake of his head, as if realizing what he'd said. "You're going to do great. Yes, of course."

"Or our names aren't Starla and Joey." Starla hooked her arm and swung it, as if overacting in a vaudeville comedy show.

"Knock 'em dead, ladies," Thompson said.

He probably wouldn't have said that if he'd known just how many times I'd had near-death encounters since I'd moved to this sleepy little sandbar town. But he didn't, so I moved on.

We parked. Jackson had followed behind us in his official police SUV. I kind of felt like the president with all the dark SUVs and security detail. In a few minutes, when I donned the media darling side of my personality and began shaking hands with people, I might actually feel like I was running for election. My campaign slogan could be *All hail the goof.*

It had a nice ring to it, right?

As the camera crew set up their equipment and production put up a tent, Starla and I met the family, the Curriers.

Frank and Tammy were in their early fifties. Frank was robust—everything from his belly, to his nose, to his loud voice. Tammy had an eighties kind of style with her big brunette hair, bold makeup, and mom jeans. Then again, the eighties were coming back in fashion, so maybe she was smart to hold onto the style. The couple had a teenage boy named Fitz.

Their charity of choice was a local fire station. Frank had been a firefighter for twenty years until he recently retired. Unlike other shows, every family that was featured got money. In fact, a ticker would run at the bottom of the screen where viewers could also donate beyond the twenty thousand the show was kicking in.

As we continued to talk to them, we learned that the family had only moved here three years ago. However, they'd always loved decorating for Christmas. That fact was evident now.

A hodgepodge of decorations surrounded us,

from blow molds to wire-frame figures to animatronic animals. Christmas music blared from speakers, and a fake snow machine shot foamy flakes into the air.

A little gingerbread booth had been set up on the corner of the property, and two elementary-aged girls gave out hot chocolate and cookies. Neighbors gathered in the streets, wearing their Christmas best and chattering happily. I even saw a couple of people exchange gifts.

It was the picture of Christmas perfection.

I took a step away from the house and mingled with the crowds, offering high fives and autographs and sage pieces of wisdom like "Don't eat yellow snow" and "When in doubt, mumble."

As my gaze scanned the roofline, I spotted a sled with Santa and his elves inside, as well as eight reindeer in front. The whole scene was illuminated by string lights. Stars had also been placed strategically around the roof.

My gaze stopped on the chimney, and I blinked, uncertain if I was seeing correctly. Everything else at the house seemed so uniform and purposeful but . . . one decoration seemed out of place amongst the rest.

I wandered over to the Curriers and pointed. "That's such a unique decoration . . . I love the way you put the naughty Santa getting stuck inside the chimney."

I actually found it odd, but I wanted to hear the story behind it. Two legs, clad in black, stuck up straight from the brick chimney.

Mrs. Currier's gaze jerked toward where I pointed, and she frowned.

"We didn't put Santa coming down into the chimney." Her face looked tense with confusion. "And a naughty Santa?" Her face went from confused to appalled. "That would be enough to cause nightmares for our smallest of visitors. We'd never do that. Mother wouldn't approve."

Guess I'd read that one wrong.

Starla, along with a cameraman, joined us.

Starla's eyelashes fluttered in confusion. "Then who do those two legs belong to?"

Mr. and Mrs. Currier exchanged a frown as they stood beside each other on the front lawn.

"I didn't put anything in the chimney," Mr. Currier said. "Did you?"

Mrs. Currier shook her head. "No, like I said, I would never want to scare children with something like that. It doesn't look festive. It looks like . . . " She swallowed hard. "Something from *The Nightmare Before Christmas*."

Starla and I exchanged a glance. I tried to keep

my expression neutral, especially since I knew the cameras were still rolling and capturing my every action.

"Maybe Fitz put something up there as a joke. Fitz!" Mr. Currier's voice boomed. "Come over here for a second!"

Their son wandered over. He was probably seventeen or eighteen, twenty pounds overweight, and had a buzz cut that did nothing to enhance his features.

When he looked at Starla, I could tell by the way his eyes brightened that he was crushing on her. He didn't have to say or do anything for that point to be clear. His eyes lit up like a little boy . . . wait for it . . . on Christmas day.

Man, I was good.

"Fitz." Mr. Currier's voice hardened. "Do you know anything about the legs in the chimney?"

Fitz pulled his gaze away from Starla for long enough to look on top of the roof. "Legs? In the chimney? Why would I do that? You know I hate heights."

"So you know nothing about this?" Mr. Currier's tone took on the tone of a stern father, all his Christmas cheer seeming to disappear. "You didn't put a mannequin up there as a joke? I know you wanted to do a dark humor Christmas theme."

Fitz pulled his gaze back over toward his father,

skimming Starla again as he did. "No, Father. I know nothing about that."

His voice sounded a little too saccharine. Was that because he was lying? Or was he just trying to get under his father's skin?

I looked back at Jackson at that moment. When I saw the frown on his face, I knew exactly what he was thinking—that I had found trouble . . . again.

And he may have been right.

But the only thing going through my mind was a re-written version of "Up on the Housetop." Except my lyrics went something like this:

Down through the chimney with lots of ploy.

Because that man's a Christmas decoy.

Click here to continue reading.

ALSO BY CHRISTY BARRITT:

THE WORST DETECTIVE EVER

I'm not really a private detective. I just play one on TV.

Joey Darling, better known to the world as Raven Remington, detective extraordinaire, is trying to separate herself from her invincible alter ego. She played the spunky character for five years on the hit TV show *Relentless*, which catapulted her to fame and into the role of Hollywood's sweetheart. When her marriage falls apart, her finances dwindle to nothing, and her father disappears, Joey finds herself on the Outer Banks of North Carolina, trying to piece together her life away from the limelight. But as people continually mistake her for the character she played on TV, she's tasked with solving real life crimes . . . even though she's terrible at it.

ABOUT THE AUTHOR

USA Today has called Christy Barritt's books "scary, funny, passionate, and quirky."

Christy writes both mystery and romantic suspense novels that are clean with underlying messages of faith. Her books have sold more than three million copies and have won the Daphne du Maurier Award for Excellence in Suspense and Mystery, have been twice nominated for the Romantic Times Reviewers' Choice Award, and have finaled for both a Carol Award and Foreword Magazine's Book of the Year.

She is married to her Prince Charming, a man who thinks she's hilarious—but only when she's not trying to be. Christy is a self-proclaimed klutz, an avid music lover who's known for spontaneously bursting into song, and a road trip aficionado.

When she's not working or spending time with her family, she enjoys singing, playing the guitar, and exploring small, unsuspecting towns where people have no idea how accident-prone she is.

Find Christy online at:
www.christybarritt.com
www.facebook.com/christybarritt
www.twitter.com/cbarritt

Sign up for Christy's newsletter to get information on all of her latest releases here: **www.christybarritt. com/newsletter-sign-up/**

facebook.com / AuthorChristyBarritt
twitter.com / christybarritt
instagram.com / cebarritt